NO WEAPON BUT HIS FACE!

A shaggy mane of greasy, tangled black locks fell over the creature's ears and down its neck. The red of its eyes gleamed in the candlelight off two sharp, fanglike canine teeth. A smear of bright blood stretched across the creature's mouth and chin and the thing flicked its thick tongue, licking a few gleaming drops from its fangs.

With a frighteningly quick motion, the creature threw itself down on all fours and its obscene tongue lapped blood from one of the pools on the floor.

"Delicious," the creature said to Cal. "Don't you agree?"

*Books in the RUNESWORD series
from Ace*

RUNESWORD VOLUME ONE: OUTCASTS
RUNESWORD VOLUME TWO: SKRYLING'S BLADE
RUNESWORD VOLUME THREE: THE DREAMSTONE
RUNESWORD VOLUME FOUR: HORRIBLE HUMES
RUNESWORD VOLUME FIVE: DARK DIVIDE

RUNESWORD VOLUME SIX: THE STONE OF TIME
(Coming in March)

Volume Five
DARK DIVIDE

Mark Acres

ACE BOOKS, NEW YORK

This book is an Ace original edition,
and has never been previously published.

RUNESWORD: DARK DIVIDE

An Ace Book / published by arrangement with
Bill Fawcett and Associates

PRINTING HISTORY
Ace edition / October 1991

ISBN: 0-441-73698-X

Ace Books are published by The Berkley Publishing Group,
200 Madison Avenue, New York, New York 10016.
The name "ACE" and the "A" logo
are trademarks belonging to Charter Communications, Inc.

PRINTED IN THE UNITED STATES OF AMERICA

10 9 8 7 6 5 4 3 2 1

This is for Bill,
who let me write it,
and Jamie,
who helped
more than she knows.

PROLOGUE

"Ow!"

The orc growled with pain. Once again he'd scraped his fat thigh on the jagged rock outcroppings. He reached down to check for blood, but couldn't worm his hand down his side. The passageway was too narrow.

The panting creature raised his arms high over his head and twisted his whole body hard; first left, then right. With a final heave, he freed himself from the tight turn in the cavern tunnel and lunged suddenly forward.

"Unnh! Ow! Ooh!"

The orc howled as his foot struck a large stone and sent it flying forward. He grabbed his stubbed toe and hopped up and down on his aching leg. The stone clattered as it rolled forward, then pinged several times as it bounced down the sides of a sharp drop-off just ahead.

"A thousand curses on Gutstomper!" the orc muttered, stopping his dance of pain to peer into the black abyss that gaped before him. Down the drop-off went, far into the very bowels of the forbidden mountain. There was a way down, though. It looked difficult, steep, and dangerous to the orc, even for one as surefooted beneath the earth as himself. He would have to make that difficult climb to fulfill his mission. But first he would rest himself and have a bite to eat.

The orc, Bloodseeker by name, settled his bulk on the tunnel floor by the drop-off. Carefully he placed his wooden spear by his side. An orc couldn't be too cautious in an unknown place—even a place that men and elves never visited. He checked his wooden shield, which had been fitted with iron reinforcing bars. Had it cracked? No, no. That was good. His fine steel dagger was in its sheath on his belt as well. Good.

Finally, before allowing himself the pleasure of food, Bloodseeker checked the large leather pouch that hung from the right side of his belt. From it he withdrew a small black glass vial, its stopper sealed in place with wax. For the hundredth time in his eight days of wandering beneath the earth, the orc made certain the vial was safe. Gingerly, he replaced it in the pouch and leaned back carefully so that the vial would not scrape against the stone wall or floor.

"Now me eat in peace, and Gutstomper and his orders be tortured by the Dark Lord!" Bloodseeker shouted into the silent darkness. From his large rucksack, Bloodseeker took a dried, cured human thighbone. The sounds of his biting, chewing, and slurping drifted through the tunnels and caverns, while more curses on Gutstomper drifted through his mind.

It was a fool's errand the orc chieftain had sent him on; a fool's errand, and worse, one that involved difficult work. Let Gutstomper himself make the trip to the Ochre Mountain! Let him trudge for eight days or more in this endless maze, searching for one particular piece of worthless granite rock! Let him worry about carrying some fragile glass bottle while he climbed and scrambled and slid and rolled along in these forsaken passageways, where not even a straying human could be hunted for food!

"Me a fool to come here," Bloodseeker told himself, and knew it was true. For it was not only elves and humans who avoided the Ochre Mountain. Not even the orcs of Bloodseeker's tribe, who lived in the foothills in the mountain's shadow, were allowed to trespass on its soil, on pain of death. Why this was so, no orc now remembered. But there were stories.

The mountain orcs said that the Ochre Mountain was named for its peculiar color, a mottled mixture of greens, browns, and yellows. Seen from a distance, the range of peaks looked the color of the putrid stuff that oozed from unhealed wounds. They said that a long time ago, so long ago that Bloodseeker's mother's mother's mother could not remember it. There was a fearsome battle between the orcs, on one side, and elves and men on the other. The fighting raged for days, and the orcs were on the verge of victory, when corrupt elven magic struck an untold fearsome blow that left the orcs, and many of the men as well, hideously wounded, crippled, and dying. The dead were stripped and left, and the putrescence of first their wounds and then their bodies seeped into the earth, discoloring the entire mountain. Not even the disgusting elves would claim the land after that. Instead, they left it, naming it something in their own tongue that meant "Bloody Range."

There were other stories, too. There were stories of strange, powerful magic left buried beneath the mountain. It was said there were creatures beneath the earth who thrived on the countless rotting bodies on the ground above them. Some said there were molding, shuffling dwellers beneath the mountain, things to whom death meant nothing but a kind of new life. . . .

"Yes, me fool to come here," Bloodseeker muttered again, pausing in his repast as his own thoughts made him grow colder with fear. Gutstomper, the tribal chieftain, had ordered him to violate the taboo, to carry the glass vial into the heart of the Ochre Mountain, but Gutstomper hated Bloodseeker. Maybe Gutstomper had sent Bloodseeker to die among things that lived while dead. . . .

"Ah, but reward!" Bloodseeker reminded himself. "Reward promised by great wizard!" Yes, yes, he thought, even Gutstomper had cringed on the day the giant wizard had visited the tribe, bearing with him the vial that now rested in Bloodseeker's leather pouch. The wizard had promised great rewards to the entire tribe if one orc were brave enough to do him an errand; a little errand, really. There would be battles, the wizard said, battles with elves and men. And he, the great wizard, would aid the orcs with flying beasts and powerful magic. Men and elves would fall in battle like wheat before scythes! the wizard said. There would be blood and meat aplenty, and booty, too. After their victory, orcs would never need fear men again!

"Gutstomper smart," Bloodseeker mused. Yes, smart enough to see that such reward would not be easily earned, no matter what the wizard said. The "errand" the wizard wanted would be very risky indeed. And so Gutstomper had wisely picked Bloodseeker to carry out that errand. He, Bloodseeker, who stood next in line to be chieftain when Gutstomper was dead. If Bloodseeker died beneath the forbidden mountain, Gutstomper would remain blameless and secure in his power. If Bloodseeker succeeded and returned, it would be Gutstomper who could claim the glory, for he, the great chieftain, had chosen the warrior to carry out the wizard's task.

"Yes, Gutstomper plenty smart," Bloodseeker whispered to himself. "But maybe not smart as Bloodseeker!" For when Bloodseeker returned—successful, victorious in his quest to the forbidden mountain—who among the orcs could deny him anything? And who would raise a hand to protect Gutstomper when Bloodseeker rammed a spear through the fat chieftain's belly, driving it up through the hated orc's chest and throat and brain until it popped out through the top of his skull? No one. Then Bloodseeker would be chieftain!

"Me be chieftain, and Gutstomper be food for worms," Bloodseeker said aloud to the empty blackness. "Me be chieftain! Me slaughter elves and men! Me find favor with the great wizard! Me be servant to none, and lord of all I see!"

But that, Bloodseeker was forced to remind himself, would be later. That would be after he had found the strange slab of granite described to him by the wizard, and poured the contents of the strange vial into the hole in that particular piece of rock.

Bloodseeker heaved a sigh, looked down the drop-off before him, and tossed the now-bare thighbone down into the darkness. Maybe, he thought, maybe the wizard had told the truth. Maybe this was a simple errand, even if it did involve a lot of climbing and trudging and slithering around in narrow passageways. After all, orcs were at home beneath the ground. There was no danger here from men or elves, and, so far as Bloodseeker could see, no danger from anything else. Well, if it was a simple errand, so much the better. He'd get it done, then go back to kill Gutstomper.

Bloodseeker lay on his bulging belly and gradually lowered himself feetfirst over the ledge. His feet kicked against the side of the drop-off until first one, then the other, found a purchase. Then, with feet and fat hands grabbing, grasping, and scraping against every tiny outcropping in cliff side, the orc climbed slowly down.

He climbed for one hour, then another. The thick black fluid that orcs call blood oozed from his palms, fingers, thighs, and pricklish snout. His muscles trembled from weariness. But still the drop-off led him down, down, down, ever deeper.

Bloodseeker feared his strength would fail before he reached the bottom of the pit, but at last his feet touched a flat, smooth floor. The orc collapsed, exhausted, onto his back. His head lolled from side to side and his eyes saw he was in yet another tunnel system.

"So far down, must be close," Bloodseeker mumbled to himself. He staggered to his feet and pressed forward, taking the nearest passageway for several hundred paces. Then he suddenly stopped, sucking in air with a gasp of amazement.

Before him opened the greatest underground chamber he had ever seen. The huge room was roughly circular, more than a crossbow bolt's range in diameter. Its ceiling arched out of his sight above. But whether it was a natural cavern or hewn from rock over centuries by the labor of thousands of hands, Bloodseeker could not tell. At least part of the room was created by design, for at the far side was an enormous stone staircase, clearly hewn by intention, leading upward for some two, no, three hundred steps to a great stone throne. At the foot of the stairs was an altar stone, its sides long stained with the bloodshed of ages of use. Around the walls of the room were carefully spaced ledges, which could serve as platforms for sitting or standing. The cavern looked like a great circular theater, with the altar stone at the front and the throne above it as its natural focal points.

But the room was not the sole source of Bloodseeker's wonder. Most remarkable of all was the smooth, cylindrical slab of granite in the center of the room. It reached down from the unseen darkness of the ceiling above and plunged into the floor of the room, like a giant granite stake impaling the earth itself.

"This be place," Bloodseeker whispered into the stillness. "But what kind place?"

What kind of place, indeed? Though long deserted, the room seemed to pulse with a kind of life that was not life, with a cold nonlife from an age long forgotten. Bloodseeker's heart raced like a scared human's. His stubby, bloody fingers turned cold. His tired legs trembled. As he gazed into that forbidding chamber, it seemed to Bloodseeker that the ghosts of thousands who had long ago thronged this mysterious temple screamed at him from their seats, anticipating the spilling of his blood.

Bloodseeker froze with fear.

He knew what he must do. He must cross the chamber to its center, to the giant granite slab. There he must find a small hole, and into that hole pour the mysterious contents of the vial. If he failed, he would certainly find death at the hands of Gutstomper, or perhaps a worse fate at the hands of the wizard. Yet, this place was . . .

Bloodseeker shook his head violently from side to side, as if to clear the cobwebs from his tired brain. Yes, this place was evil. What of it? He himself was evil. His whole race was evil, made, it was said, by the Dark Lord, or gods older than the Dark Lord, to war with the sickening goodness of elvenkind. What, then, need he fear?

"Evil not harm evil," Bloodseeker told himself. He took a first, hesitant step into the great chamber. "Right, evil not harm evil," he repeated. He took a second step, then a third, then finally ran full tilt toward the granite slab, eager to finish his task and be gone.

"Where hole? Where hole?" Bloodseeker panted, hopping in a circle around the stone, his eyes shifting wildly.

"There! There hole! Pour it in, pour it in!"

Bloodseeker's clumsy fingers tore the stopper from the vial, and his chubby body leaned forward to pour its meager contents into the hole. Had the orc looked more closely, he might have noticed that the hole he had found was one of several depressions visible in the otherwise smooth surface of the stone, depressions that might, to a more discerning eye, faintly suggest a skull. . . .

The orc's body froze in a combination of ecstasy and terror as the first drops of fluid from the vial spattered into the small opening in the rock. His spear clattered to the cavern floor; the nostrils in his hairy, pinkish snout flared wide. The odor of human blood exploded into the room; fresh human blood, hot and thick! But so much blood, so much! To the orc, it smelled as though he were on the edge of a veritable ocean of blood. It was beyond his understanding of things magical that the few splashes of red-black liquid he poured from the tiny vial were the concentrated essence of the blood of a hundred men or more. Those men had been slain some eight hundred years ago. Their vital essence had been trapped in the thick potion that now ate its way into the living granite.

For living it was. Or rather, something was living, of a sort, within it.

If the overwhelming scent of human blood froze Bloodseeker in ecstasy, the sight of solid granite dissolving before his eyes was terrifying. And more terrifying still was the form that was slowly emerging from the rock as it turned to powdery mist before him.

The lips were the first to emerge—thin, gray, cruel lips that formed the hole into which the liquid still flowed, as the orc continued to pour out the remaining contents of the vial. Then, through the gray rock mist that had begun to choke his lungs, Bloodseeker saw a skull form emerge from the stone, the skull form of . . .

"No! It can't be!" The orc screamed. His fat fingers dropped the vial and it crashed to the floor—too late. The work of the potion was already done, and Bloodseeker's fate was already sealed. Flesh quickly formed on the skull. In moments, a head reared itself from the stone prison on a thin white neck. High-pitched laughter erupted from the pinkening lips as almond-shaped black eyes drank in the orc's terror.

"Yes, orc," the forming face spoke. "Yes. You have helped to resurrect an elf. But not just any elf."

The roar of the explosion that followed deafened Bloodseeker. His ears rang as his body flew through the air to smash hard into the stone wall, then bounce down the series of ledges to lay on the cold floor.

"Ow! Aaaarrrgh!" Bloodseeker screamed. Knife blades of pain slashed through his body; his ribs were broken. Helpless, the orc lay on his back and feebly kicked with his legs in an attempt to crawl away. A thick cloud of gray dust from the explosion of the granite slab obscured his vision. Gradually, Bloodseeker's strength failed entirely. His legs ceased their futile effort, and he stared into the darkness. As the ringing in the orc's ears slowly faded, he heard the sound of soft footsteps approaching. Then, directly above him, a face loomed.

It was the most beautiful, evil face he had ever seen. The elf stood slightly over six feet in height. His close-cropped hair was black as jet, as were his eyes, which nevertheless seemed to glow against the background of his pale white skin. The creature's high, thin cheeks accentuated his narrow, pointed chin. His slender nose, pinched nostrils, and sneering lips completed the appearance of cunning, sinister wickedness.

"You have a rare privilege, orc," the creature hissed. "I am Malendor, the Black Elf, Lord of the Undead. You have released me from a slumber of more than seven hundred years. I thank you."

"Wu . . . wu . . ." Bloodseeker stuttered, "wizard sent me, and p-p-promise reward . . ."

"Reward you shall have indeed, orc," said Malendor. He stooped down, grasped Bloodseeker tightly around the neck, and yanked him high into the air. "Your reward shall be immortality."

Bloodseeker squealed in terror as gleaming fangs pierced the tough hide of his neck.

Gleefully, Malendor drank the blood of his first kill in more than seven centuries.

CHAPTER
1

Swordplay

"Move faster, you half-lame swaybacked nag!" the youth grumbled. His heels kicked into the ribs of the chestnut mare. "Or are you as stupid and lazy as the rest of this world of farmers and shopkeepers?"

The horse responded with a snort as she broke into a canter down the woodlands path. The animal would not willingly go any faster than that, for the path was narrow, muddy, and treacherous. Rotted dead leaves of the previous autumn still hid small rises, dips, holes, and fallen branches along the way. The tall oaks, maples, and walnuts cast long shadows that could hide countless obstacles. Neither horse nor man could see the path clearly in the cold, pale light of the setting early-spring sun.

Suddenly, the horse careened and lurched like a drunken man. The mare snorted, staggered, and nearly fell. Then she wrenched her leg free of the hole into which she'd stepped.

"Whoa, whoa, all right, then," Caltus Talienson grumbled, pulling back on the reins. "Are you injured?"

The youth sprang quickly from the back of his halted mount to examine the horse's hind legs. Neither was broken, fortunately, but there was still a chance the mare had suffered a pull or a sprain.

"Sorry, old girl," Cal said in a low, soothing voice, patting the animal's back, then affectionately rubbing her face. "No point in taking out my anger on you. Can you walk? Yes, yes, you can. Well, then, we'll go on, but I'll be easier on you."

Cal remounted and gently urged the horse forward again, this time at a slow walk, cursing himself for his unjust impatience. The mare plodded ahead contentedly. In the past weeks she had become accustomed to the human's outbursts of temper. She sensed in her instinctive animal way that his wrath was not that of an evil or malicious man, but rather that of a good soul deeply frustrated.

Noble warrior, to take out your anger on an obedient beast! thought Cal. He could only wonder what was happening to him, what strange transformation seemed to be overtaking him in recent weeks. Winter had reluctantly released its dead grip on the southlands, and the first signs of spring had appeared: leaf and bud and shoot. Spring should be a time of joy and rejoicing, a time to prepare for upcoming work and adventure, a time to shake off the lethargy of winter and set out on a bold path toward . . . what?

Who knew what, and who cared? Anything, anything would be better than this, this . . .

"Aaarrgghh!" Cal shouted out loud. He wanted to rip a tree out of the ground by its roots and use it to knock down half the forest! At least he would be doing something!

For Cal, itchy, edgy, relentless restlessness was the cause of his journey. Three days ago he had been in a small inn on the main road south to the lands near the River Drasil, trying desperately to enjoy the company of his three closest friends. He had already shared more adventure with those three than most men would hope to find in a lifetime. But his mood had made them as irritating to him as he was unpleasant to them. He could still remember every word of the stinging conversation the final night they spent together.

Bith's comments had been the most hurtful. Elizebith of Morea was the daughter of a sorceress and an increasingly powerful mage in her own right. She had been warming herself by the inn fire, her shapely figure bent slightly before the hearth. It seemed to Cal her profile pose was designed to purposely accentuate what he grudgingly admitted was a kind of attractiveness. No doubt other men thought lewd thoughts when they eyed Bith. Perhaps they wondered about the softness of her long, dark hair. Perhaps they considered how the right man could make her strange, silvery eyes shine with a girlish, romantic infatuation. Perhaps they thought other things. And didn't Bith know what men wondered? Cal just bet she did.

Not that her coy, teasing ways would ever bring her into any danger, nor even to the comeuppance she so richly deserved. Not with that red-haired, muscle-bound troll, Hathor, sitting by, a constant bodyguard. Oh, Hathor was a good sort, especially for a troll. He was brave, selfless, and powerful in battle, yet gentle in nature with his friends. But it was clear enough to Cal that any man who hoped to woo Bith would do so at peril of dissuading Hathor from his conversion to vegetarianism!

Then there was the elf, Endril, the one who started all the trouble. Maybe Endril wasn't of pure elven blood, Cal thought. Maybe he was part imp as well—at least he had been that night. Maybe that was why his own kind would have nothing to do with him. Maybe that was why he had been chosen, along with Cal, Bith, and Hathor, to do the bidding of that ungrateful fledgling god, Vili. Vili! There was a being for whom Cal had no use at all! All promises, and no rewards—that was the way of Vili.

"Ho, young Caltus Talienson," Endril had sung out over his cup of wine. The four companions had the tavern room to themselves, the other guests having long since retired. "What is that gleam in your dark, brooding eyes? Is it the firelight, glancing off your battle-hardened visage to reflect from those stern orbs? Or is it . . . Could it be? Do fiery thoughts of a human beauty burn behind your eyes?

What, I wonder, could inspire such frivolous nonsense in a hardened veteran of all your—how many?—nineteen or twenty years?" And the elf had raised a cocky eyebrow as his eyes shifted to include Bith in their field of vision.

"Huh?" Cal had answered, the elf's call barely penetrating his half-drunken thoughts, thoughts that had vanished like a dream.

"Oh ho!" Endril called out. "It is beauty that stirs the soul of this human beastie."

"What are you talking about?" Cal had answered gruffly, banging his mead cup down on the wooden table.

"You are staring at Bith. Been staring for a long time," Hathor had stated flatly.

"Oh, let him be," Bith had snapped. "Our fledgling general isn't thinking about me." Had her face reddened slightly, or was it just the heat of the fire that had made her cheeks take on a ruddiness? She had turned from the fire and seated herself on the plain wood bench next to Hathor. She took a small sip of her evening wine and looked directly at Cal. "At least, he'd better not be," she'd added.

Just like Bith to be telling people what they could or couldn't think! Cal had leaped to his feet, shouting.

"For your information, elf, there's no beauty here to turn my head. Do you take me for a, a, uh . . ." Cal's own face had flushed as he searched for a word he could use. "For one who knows nought of wenching? As for you, Hathor, I need no troll to tell me where to turn my gaze, nor, Bith, do I need an upstart witch to tell me what to think!"

"Don't you dare mention your wenching in connection with me!" Bith had fired back. "I am certainly no farm girl with nothing but a low-cut frock to recommend her. And I am neither an upstart nor a witch. Or have you forgotten, Caltus Talienson, just how much your victories in combat owe to my magic? When you think of me, think of that!"

"Cal does not think Bith pretty?" Hathor had asked, confused.

"Cal does not think of Bith at all!" Cal had roared.

"Cal does not think, period," Endril had retorted. "I intended only some gentle jesting, not a battle. Calm yourself, youth."

"Don't tell me to be calm," Cal had screamed. "That's what's wrong with you—all of you! You're calm, and why not? What do you have to look forward to? A troll and an elf whose own kind won't have anything to do with them— what's your future? And you, spellcaster, what hope do you have other than a god who uses us but never rewards us? We're all outcasts with nothing to gain. That's why Vili wanted us in the first place. Well, I'm tired of being a nobody! And nobody is going to make me continue being a nobody!"

"Perhaps you should be a somebody somewhere else," Bith had said dryly. "Go hone your combat skills with a, a . . . a wench."

"Enough," Endril had said softly, rising to his feet. "Sooner than you know, danger will be upon us. Spring is at hand, and soon armies will be able to march. The Dark Lord will try some ambitious plot against all creatures of good. We are sworn, all of us, to oppose him. This is no time for us to fall into dissension."

"More riddles and silver-tongued sylven wisdom," Cal had sneered. "I've had enough!" The youth had banged his fist on the table, rather than banging it into Endril's face.

"Then go," the elf had said in a low tone. "Go, work out your restlessness. We will await you here in seven days. Longer than that we may not have."

Cal had gone. Three days of riding through the boring lands of the south had brought him little relief. When he wasn't cursing his friends, he was cursing himself for cursing them, or taking out his frustrations on the loyal mare.

This is madness, Cal thought. I must regain control of myself. I'm behaving like a spoiled child.

So occupied was Cal with such thoughts that he hardly noticed the gradual thinning of the woods, the occasional appearance of a farmer's home, and, finally, the village in the plain a short distance ahead. It took the mare's hopeful snorting and whinnying to draw his attention to the fact that the village had an inn—and a stable.

"Right you are, girl," Cal said. "A good feed and a good night's rest for you. And as for me, I'll waste away some time drinking with the local rustics."

"So, y'see, I says to this guy, 'In'igo! You dunno what in'igo is? Iss a blue cloth,' I says, 'an' you ain't never gonna see no purtier blue cloth anywhere.' An' you know what the guy says to me?"

"I can't imagine," Cal said dully, his eyebrows raised toward the inn's low ceiling. The tavern room was packed by the time Cal had seen his horse properly stabled. The young warrior had ordered the largest tankard of ale he could get, and squeezed into the only seat left, a space at the end of a long oak table next to a fat merchant already deep in his cups. For the next half hour, Cal had been regaled with the merchant's tales of commerical victories, brilliant ploys in the constant movement of goods and coins that consumed the lives of average men.

"The guy says, he says, uh . . . I forget what he says. But it don' matter, 'cause what I did was, I sent my lackey out to bring in the sample an' show it to 'im. You always wanna show 'em a new color o' cloth. Then you can see in their eyes whether they're gonna buy or not, see?"

"Ah. Brilliant."

"You don' stay inna cloth business for thirty-three years without learning a few things like that," the old merchant gloated. "Here, lemme buy ya a drink."

Cal's tankard was empty. Perhaps another two or three, and the gentle lift of the ale would help numb the boredom of listening to this man's prattle.

"Thank you, good sir," Cal replied, "but I must insist that you let me reciprocate on the next round." Cal had learned that it was never a good thing to be in debt to a stranger, especially in a strange place.

And this inn was certainly a strange place. Nothing in its appearance was unusual; there were the usual wooden tables and benches and the large counter that served as a bar. A single stairway led to the rooms above, and a balcony overlooked the tavern room. A warm fire roared in the fireplace in the south wall. It was the crowd that Cal thought strange.

Tomorrow was neither a rest day nor a feast day, yet the tavern was filled to overflowing, and most of the customers were locals. Cal scanned the room again as the merchant ordered more drinks. The bulk of those here were local farmers, artisans, and tradesmen, judging by their clothing and the snippets of conversation Cal could overhear. Oddly, nearly a third present were females. Cal judged most to be wives and daughters accompanying husbands and fathers; two were women whose virtue could be had for a silver coin. There were the usual few travelers and drifters: a seeming holy man who kept to himself even in the midst of the crowd, and smirked at the rowdy behavior around him; a pair of men who must be mercenaries searching for employment; four gnomes who sat to the side at a tiny table provided by the innkeeper for the occasional wee folk who visited; the merchant and his company of lackeys and guards.

What, Cal wondered, would cause so many local folk to be rowdily drinking on this night? Their daily chores would call them from sleep long before sunrise.

"Now, then, what was I saying?" The merchant's drunken query intruded on Cal's thoughts.

"You were telling me," Cal said, lifting his tankard for a deep swig, "why a fine merchant, like yourself, needs, let's see, how many do you have? I make it, ten armed retainers. Why such a guard when you're traveling in this peaceful land?" Cal drank deep, then lowered his tankard and smiled a mock drunk smile at the man.

"Ah, yes. Well, that's because—"

"Because of the bloody bandits, and all the other weird goings-on that are going to be the death of this village," broke in the farmer who had heretofore sat quietly on Cal's left.

"Be quiet, Peter," hissed another farmer from down the table. "These outsiders will be gone tomorrow. Leave our business to ourselves. Don't mention evil and you won't invite it."

"Nothing mysterious about the evil around here, I assure you," the merchant said, rising to his feet to address the table. "There'sh nothing here to fear; Rafael, the rich, is here! Hah hah! I'm a 'sperienced traveler, an' I've seen ban'its before. My guards here can take care of 'em."

The fool, Cal thought. The inn had fallen silent during Rafael's speech, and not a single eye had missed his fat hand patting his full coin pouch as he spoke. He would be lucky to live out the night if there were but one desperate man in the crowd.

The silence was broken by a low, threatening voice from the table behind Cal's. The voice spoke slowly and distinctly; the speaker clearly wanted every word to make an impression.

"Your guards aren't worth the water this ale will be in an hour."

Rafael turned to face the speaker, nearly tripping over the bench as he did so.

"And jus' who are you, to deni . . . to deni . . . to insult my guards, you ruffian?"

"I'm the man who should be your guard, good sir. My companion and I are the only guards you need. If you'll give me your leave, in five minutes' time we'll be the only guards you have."

Cal studied the man as he spoke. He stood a full six feet in height and was stockily built, with broad, muscled shoulders. He held himself erect like a soldier. The scar running down his craggy face from his left eye to his grizzled salt-and-pepper beard told he was experienced. Clearly he was bold: his hard green eyes stared straight ahead as he spoke, and not a nerve twitched, though he was ready to spring into action. Still, the man was old, forty if a day, Cal judged. His tattered, padded tunic and greasy, gray hair indicated recent hard times.

His companion looked only slightly younger. He was thinner, shorter, perhaps more swift? And more nervous.

Cal saw his eyes darting from his friend to the crowd and back, and his hand nervously clasping, then unclasping around his large ale mug.

Clatters, thuds, and oaths answered the man's speech. Two of Rafael's guard, their pride stung, overturned benches and drinkers in their clumsy haste to get to their feet.

"A hundred devils eat you, you scum!" shouted the first angry, drunken guard. "You insult my honor, and you will die!"

With a roar the guard took one lumbering, giant step up onto the table before him, producing a dagger from his boot as he did so.

"My sword! My sword!" bellowed the second guard at one of the merchant's lackeys. "Don't kill him, Marco! Leave some for me!"

The big man stood his ground, staring straight into the eyes of his first foe. His hands dropped slowly down toward the table before him, and Cal noticed for the first time the long bundle of brown cloth those hands sought.

"Marco, sit down, sit down," Rafael muttered. His fear of an ugly incident was overcoming his drunkenness.

"A fight! A fight!" roared the crowd. A few men helped the women toward the inn door, but the bulk of the crowd stood and fanned out to form a large circle in front of the fireplace. Benches and tables were quickly shoved aside to make room for men to fight. The innkeeper's cries of alarm were ignored. The four gnomes scampered from their little table, and in a twinkling had themselves seated on the main counter that served as a bar, chattering merrily among themselves at the prospect of violence between the humans.

"Come, Rafael," Cal said cheerily, his own aspect brightened. He clapped the older man around the shoulder and guided him to the edge of the circle. "Let's see what your guards can do against this fellow."

Through it all, the big man stood his ground, and his smaller companion remained seated, his eyes darting around the circle of the crowd, but his hands making no move to produce a weapon.

"If you seek death, fool," the large man said, his eyes burning into Marco's, "you have found it. Come for me!"

With a roar, the guard Marco pounced from the tabletop, his dagger raised high to plunge into the big man's breast. He did not reach the floor alive.

As the guard sprung from the tabletop, the big man's left hand flipped back the brown cloth before him, and his right grasped a gleaming bastard sword. With one smooth, lightning move, the man raised the sword, circled it to his right, brought it down to chest height, and swung it level before him. The blade cleaved Marco's flying body cleanly in half. The dead man's severed legs dropped to the floor; his head and torso landed on the table before the swordsman. Amazement showed in his dying eyes, and his lips sputtered a croak of surprise and a spray of blood.

The big man kicked over the table with its grisly burden, sending mugs and tankards flying into the crowd. He gripped his sword two handed now, holding it at an upward angle, straight out in front of his chest. Knees bent slightly forward, he circled slowly and eyed the crowd.

"Who's next?" he challenged.

A low murmur rippled through the spectators. Cal's dark eyes grew wide with excitement; his heart began to pound, and his face flushed slightly. For he had heard the soft, high note of that sword as it sliced through air and cloth and flesh. Even now, as firelight danced off the shining blade, blood and gore still dripping from it, he saw the powerful, magical runes that ran the four and a half feet of its length, from hilt to point. It was a runesword, one of those rare, enchanted weapons through which the god Vili could manifest himself. He who wielded such a blade was near invincible in personal combat. More, the possession of a runesword was linked in some mysterious way with success against the Dark Lord. Cal knew in an instant that at whatever price, he must obtain that sword.

"How about you?" the big man called again, thrusting the sword in the direction of Marco's companion. The guard stood still, hesitating. The lackey had returned with his sword, but Marco's death had cleared the guard's head enough for him to know he did not want to join his friend.

"Here, here, friend," Rafael called to the swordsman. "There's no need for this . . . bloodshed. What is it you want? A job? Well . . . well, uh, it seems I have an opening—"

"Be silent, you bloated, croaking frog. I'm not in your employ yet. When I am, I'll take orders with respect. But now, I want to see if there are any men in this place!" Not once had the swordsman broken his stance. His companion, seated on a bench that now stood incongruously before the overturned table, still eyed the crowd warily, keeping particular watch, Cal noted, on the swordsman's back.

"Nonsense," Cal found himself saying nonchalantly. "The opening created by Marco's sudden death is already filled. By me. Rafael, would you care to have me remove this fellow, so we may get on with our merrymaking?" Cal's dark eyes met the swordsman's and their gazes locked.

"Now, now, young man . . ." Rafael began.

"Who are you?" Cal shouted at the swordsman, his face suddenly grim and serious.

"Hah!" The swordsman's face broke into a wicked grin. "What's this? A stripling, one with more spirit than brains. Go home, boy. I don't like killing children."

"I asked your name. I expect an answer," Cal replied in a low, icy tone.

"Who do you think you are to ask?" the big man taunted back.

"I am Caltus Talienson, hero of Cairngorm, leader of the men of Steadfast-by-Sea. I have defeated foes and friends from beyond the Dark Lord's Mistwall, and I am the one who is asking you your name, you stupid, murderous sot."

"Agan!" the swordsman called to his companion, his dark brows rising in mock fear. "Throw this whelp a sword so he can die armed. Know, then, Caltus Talienson, I am Gunther Stedfyrd, your better, and your death!"

With one smooth motion, Agan stood, produced a long sword and scabbard from beneath his cloak, and gracefully tossed it toward Cal. The youth caught the scabbard high in the air in his left hand, and the ring of steel sounded as he drew the sword with his right.

"Fifteen pieces of silver on Gunther," cried one of the gnomes. "Any takers?"

Only silence greeted the gnome's offer.

"I'll take that bet," Cal said coldly, never taking his eyes from Gunther's. "The money is in my coin purse. You'll have to trust me for it, friend gnome, for at the moment I need my hands at the ready."

"You're on," the gnome replied cheerily. "I'm sure Gunther will let me strip your body for a just debt."

"No doubt. But before you count your money, I'd be certain this is a fair fight," Cal said. "Gunther, tell your friend Agan there to stand aside."

Gunther smiled and nodded. Agan drifted back to the edge of the circle of men.

"There, boy. Now, if you're so eager to die, come for me!"

Cal raised the long sword, his arms spread wide to his sides, and began to slowly circle. There was no point in normal sword fighting. Cal knew that one blow from the runesword would pass right through any normal blade, and his body as well. He also knew that Gunther would most likely swing from right to left. If Cal could get that bench on his own left . . .

"Come on, boy. This is tiresome." Gunther feinted a lunge toward Cal, hoping to draw the lad in. Cal stood his ground, still circling slowly. He continued his cautious movement until the bench, where Agan had sat, was about five feet away to his left.

Then Cal suddenly lunged forward—his own feint. As he expected, Gunther swiftly raised the runesword, drawing back to strike one mighty, fatal blow. Cal waited until Gunther finished his backswing and the sword was, for an instant, motionless. Then the youth threw himself backward, headfirst, to his own left. With his right hand he flipped the worthless long sword toward Gunther's face, not to do harm, but to distract and disorient the large man.

The sweet singing of the runesword cleaving empty air sounded inches from Cal's face as the youth hung in the air, horizontal. The deadly edge passed swiftly just over his body, and then Cal crashed to the floor. He was rolling as he hit, his arms reaching for the wooden bench.

Gunther's sword blow smashed into the inn floor. The magic blade bit into the wood to a depth of six inches. Gunther yanked back on the hilt of the weapon, eager to prepare for another strike.

But he was too slow. Cal came to his feet with the bench in his arms like a huge awkward club, and before Gunther could raise his sword, Cal swung. The blow caught Gunther behind the knees and sent the man sprawling forward, the runesword popping from his grasp. Cal raised the bench again and crashed it down, end first, into Gunther's spine and ribs.

Gunther made a sound that was something between a groan and a shout of rage. He rolled over, only to let out a high-pitched scream. His back was broken.

Cal seized the runesword and raised the blade high over Gunther's chest. He could see the surprise and the pain in his foe's eyes.

"Now, tell me, Gunther Stedfyrd," Cal said in a hoarse whisper, "where you obtained such an enchanted blade, and I will let you live. Do not lie to me, for I know what this weapon truly is."

"How that blade came to me is no concern of yours," Gunther grunted between clenched teeth. "But be warned: magic and overconfidence are no match for quickness and skill. Now, end this, boy. I can hardly bear the pain."

Obviously the man was hopelessly crippled. Better for a fighting man to die in battle than to be an invalid for life, Cal thought. He plunged the blade downward, and Gunther's eyes went dim.

"Nooooo!"

The scream was from Agan, who was already running, dagger in hand, straight at Cal. Cal jerked the magic blade, amazingly light, from Gunther's body. Even with his quick reflexes, he barely had the blade level when Agan, running too quickly to stop, hurled himself at Cal. It was a foolish move; the man impaled himself upon the sword. He was dead before the forward momentum of his body brought his head to rest atop Cal's hands on the hilt.

Cal wrenched the sword free, letting Agan's body fall next to Gunther's. He drew a deep breath, then turned around, facing again toward the bar.

"Innkeeper! My good friend, the gnome there, will buy drinks for the house!"

Cal drank deep that night, overjoyed at obtaining so rare a prize with such ease. Drunkenly, he wondered what adventures and dangers were ahead, for never did a runesword enter his life, but the Dark Lord's plots and countless dangers followed.

CHAPTER
2

Nightfall

"Ooh," Cal groaned as he trotted along the side of the column, checking the spacing of Rafael's guards. "By the gods, what a head I've got today."

Ale had flowed, and wine, and mead, and a strange brew made of soured mash, and there had been talk of battles and leadership and great rewards, and a deal had been cut, and now . . .

"Oh, trouble," Cal told himself. Sometime shortly before sunrise, he had agreed to see Rafael's column, now short one guard, to Dralton, a major commercial city of the southlands, where Rafael maintained his rich household. The city was only two days' travel to the east, but that would put Cal five days away from his rendezvous with Endril, Bith, and Hathor. He would have to cover the distance in only two.

But, Cal cheered himself as he fought down a rumbling lurch in this stomach, I'll have something to tell them about! And something for Endril to ponder as well. A runesword! Such a prize! And while Cal did not doubt that eventually the blade would have to be destroyed (such was always the fate of Vili's runeswords, it seemed), its mere possession gave him and his friends a great advantage in any coming conflict with the minions of the Dark Lord, whatever form that conflict might take.

Still, Cal was troubled by his own folly the previous night. He had moved too soon. He knew nothing now of Gunther Stedfyrd, or how the mercenary fighter had come to possess this sword. Worse, in the celebration following his fight with Gunther, he had completely forgotten about the farmer Peter's words. What strange things had afflicted the village? What details could be learned about the bandits they feared?

There had been no time to follow up on these questions. Sunrise came, it seemed, only moments after Cal shut his eyes. Within the hour, Rafael's column was on the road, with Cal, the newly hired leader of the guard, in command.

As for Rafael, he had sobered quickly enough after only two hours' sleep. When not in his cups, he was a different man, indeed. He knew the count of every item on every mule, the distance to be covered, the road to be taken, the type of terrain ahead. He conveyed this information to Cal quickly and concisely, paid him in advance for two days' wages, and then retired to his litter with the curtains drawn, no doubt to snooze away most of the day.

The road to Dralton was muddy, and the pack mules contrary, but Cal had few real complaints about his temporary task. He was commanding men again! While guarding a merchant's party was hardly glamorous, it was something to do. Something fairly easy in this country. The road wound its way up and down the gently rolling hills, passing between cleared farm fields and meadows. In the pale spring sunlight Cal surveyed the muddy, brown-green fields, dotted here and there by bursts of yellow, gold, red, and blue from the season's first flowers. There were few places for ambushers to hide, he noted. The hung-over guard commander stopped for a moment to drink in the cool spring air and enjoy the simple beauty of the countryside.

Nevertheless, Cal was taking no chances. He had two men scouting about a thousand yards ahead, and two trailing the column from the same distance to the rear. The remaining five guards rode alongside Rafael's hand-carried litter in the center. The twenty-odd pack animals, tended by lackeys, were spaced ahead of and behind the litter. Cal's own position was at the head of the main column. Occasionally, as now, he trotted up and down the column's length, checking.

Satisfied with his inspection, Cal rode back toward the head of the column. In his imagination, he relived his victory over Gunther Stedfyrd, relishing the boldness and cleverness of his own tactics. It was sad, of course, that Gunther had had to die. But the big man had sought the conflict, and death was the constant hazard of the professional soldier.

As Cal passed the lead mule to take his own position, he saw that the column was approaching a good-sized hill, higher than the others they had crossed. His scouts were out of sight, over the crest. Odd, though, that one of the pair hadn't waited at the hilltop to maintain contact, Cal thought. Still, these guards were not of the best quality. They lacked discipline and training. If he could command them for only a few weeks . . .

The bowman appeared from nowhere. One instant the road before Cal was empty; the next, the man was standing there, grinning. By instinct, not thought, Cal raised his shield, and the longbow shaft thunked into it with such violent force that Cal was thrown form his mount!

"Guards! Two men to the front," Cal cried, rolling and leaping to his feet, his right hand drawing the feather-light runesword.

A second arrow whizzed past his head, a near miss despite the speed of his movement. That bowman was good! And he was still about fifty yards away. If Cal charged him on foot, he'd have time for a another shot. . . .

"Caltus, Caltus, help! They are upon us!"

Cal looked back to see the column scattering in disarray. A swarm of ragged cutthroats hacked and slashed their way through guards and lackeys alike. Rafael was standing near his litter, screaming for aid. While Cal watched, helpless, the merchant was taken from behind by a short, swarthy man who neatly slit the fat man's throat. The ruffian threw the body to the ground, then paused to spit in the dead man's face.

No time, no time . . .

Cal whirled with a roar of rage, whipping the great runesword through the air in broad circles before him as he charged the bowman. Already the skilled bandit was drawing another arrow. Cal's feet churned the muddy earth as he ran forward, his loud battle cry drowning out all other sounds in his own ears. He was forty yards away, thirty yards . . . The bandit nocked the arrow, drew back the bowstring . . .

With a great sidearm swing, Cal let fly the huge runesword! The stunned bowman held his string for an instant, and it was an instant too long. The magic blade pierced his sternum and slid through his body with a sickening, slicing sound. The bandit flew backward a full five yards before his body flopped to rest, impaled on the damp hillside by the enchanted blade.

"Yaaaahhh!" Cal shouted, his battle lust fully aroused. He ran to retrieve his weapon. Grabbing the sword from the ground, Cal slashed downward, severing the bandit's head. Then Cal whistled twice, sharply, for his mount. In seconds he was back on his horse, heading toward the main body of the column.

One guard, who had somehow escaped the mayhem, rode toward him.

"Cal, Cal, what do we do?" the guard called, reining to a halt beside the youthful leader.

"We earn our pay! Turn and charge by my side!"

Ten seconds later the two men galloped into a confused melee. Cal lost all track of his companion. He saw only red before his eyes, the red of rage and blood. The ring of steel and the high-pitched whine of the runesword filled his ears as he slashed left and right, cutting down one, then, two, soon four, then five men—and found he had ridden completely through the fight. He yanked the reins hard to the left to turn for another run, and dug his heels into the chestnut's flanks.

The goodly mare started to spring forward and stopped suddenly. Cal lurched from his saddle, barely able to stay on the horse. As he struggled to regain his seat, foul breath assaulted his nostrils, and a hideous creature wrapped strong arms around the mare's neck.

The thing was the size of a man, perhaps five feet eight inches tall, with wild, greasy black hair sticking out of its head in all directions. Its naked gray skin was filthy, caked with mud. Its sharp, jagged teeth were littered with bloody flesh, and its black eyes were cold with lifeless rage against all things living. With one powerful twist, it broke the horse's neck. Cal heard a horrid crack. The dead mount collapsed on its knees. With a shout, Cal tumbled headlong into the mud.

The thing was on him quickly. Without time even to stand, Cal rolled onto his back and thrust upward with the great sword, running the blade through the disgusting creature's neck. With a flick of his wrist, Cal finished his work. The filthy thing's head toppled off to the right.

Cal gasped as he stood, too breathless for the moment to charge back into the bloody melee where once the column had been.

Then he realized the creature he had just killed was laughing.

He looked around to see the stocky body, still standing, reach down and pick up the hideous, laughing head. Then the great arm raised and hurled the head straight at Cal's chest!

The thing's ragged, sharp teeth hooked around the links in Cal's chain-mail shirt. Its jaws worked furiously as the slavering beast tried to eat its way through the quilted tunic beneath the armor.

Cal screamed in horror. He grabbed the head by the hair with his free left hand and pulled—in vain. The teeth were locked around the mail links. . . .

Huge arms tightened around Cal from behind. A terrible chill ran through his body, as though his blood had suddenly lost all its heat. Cal's vision fogged; the world grew gray, then black, as the breath was squeezed from his lungs and the life force drained from his body.

CHAPTER
3

Yvaine

There was darkness for a long time. Darkness and nothingness.

Then there was cold. There was no light, just cold. The cold invaded Cal's feet, ankles, legs, fingers, hands, and arms. It felt like the cold of death.

Then there was the goddess, and light for an instant, and warmth and pain. Then there was nothingness again.

The goddess was good. She came bringing light and warmth again and again. But there was pain, always the pain. And always the dark nothingness returned.

Cal dreamed.

The goddess came out of a brilliant light, calling him to her. She was fair and comely, so beautiful Cal could hardly breathe when he looked upon her. Yet she smiled and caressed his face and told him to come with her. Then Cal trembled violently as alien, evil thoughts filled him. His skin turned a sickly, mottled gray. His eyes burned with an evil lust, and a hideous hunger overcame him. He reached out to embrace the goddess, drew her into his arms, and, reaching up with his huge, powerful, rotting hands, snapped her thin white neck. . . .

"Unnnhhh!"

"Shh. Be at peace, Caltus Talienson. You only dream. It is only a dream. Can you awaken?"

"Unnnhhh," Cal replied, fighting to open his eyes. Pain gripped his chest, and his limbs felt unnaturally cold. "Goddess . . . danger . . . ," Cal muttered.

"It is time to awaken, Caltus. Can you wake yourself?" The voice of the goddess was firm, insistent.

Light stabbed Cal's eyes as they finally fluttered open. He turned his head, wincing, and the pain shot through his chest again.

"Your wound heals slowly, and you are very weak. You must wake up long enough to take nourishment."

"Unnnhhh."

Cal allowed the goddess to force-feed him a few swallows of a hot meat broth, then returned to his fitful slumbers.

It came back to him in one sudden, painful flash of memory. The bowman on the road, the sudden attack, the destruction of the column, the hideous beast-man that had thrown its own head at him! And the sword—where was the runesword?

Cal opened his eyes and tossed back the coverlets of silk and fur. Bright sunlight glistened off the white plastered walls, causing him to blink. He listened intently. Street sounds drifted to him through the open arched doorway to the balcony. Cal shivered; the spring air was still cool. Wherever he was, the place belonged to someone of wealth. Cal scanned the tapestry on the far wall and decided it alone was worth more than a month's wages for a working artisan.

The youth propped himself up in the bed and winced with the pain of his chest wounds. As he moved, a foul black fluid oozed onto his white linen bandages. He must not be healing very well. . . .

"At last you're awake. And sitting up some, I see. You must be better today."

Cal looked up to see the goddess of his recent dreams standing in the doorway to his chamber, framed as if in a portrait. Long, golden curls cascaded down to frame her thin face before caressing her small but squared shoulders. Her face was dominated by large blue eyes that sparkled in the morning sunlight. Her cheekbones were high, her nose small with just enough upturn to indicate a certain stubborn perkiness. Her lips were thin but full colored, and her fair skin touched lightly with freckles.

Cal noticed her diminutive, boyish form as she walked across the room. Then her flowing blue gown began to cling to her figure, and his attention was drawn to her firm breasts and the outline of her clearly feminine legs. She walked with grace; flashes of stories he had heard about beautiful ladies at the courts of kings started to run through Cal's befuddled mind.

"You have caused me much concern, Caltus Talienson," she said, smiling in a strange way that could be perfectly innocent or could be seen as outrageous flirtation. She reached out her rather large, thin hand and ran the backs of her long nails gently down the side of Cal's cheek. "Your face is cool now. The fever has broken. This is a good sign."

"Who are you?" Cal whispered, forgetting to close his mouth when he had finished speaking.

"Forgive me, Caltus. I forgot that you had not met me. I am Yvaine, daughter of Rafael, the merchant, who was slain in the attack in which you were wounded. Has your memory returned to you?"

"Uh, yes," Cal replied, red shame creeping up his pale face. He was not likely to forget his complete failure in what should have been the simple task of guarding a man and a few pack mules.

"You blush, Caltus. But there is no need for shame. You fought well and bravely."

"I should have been better prepared, and I should have known that. . . . How do you know all this?"

"I was there."

Cal sank back into the soft bed, exhausted and confused. He could not remember this girl at the battle. Or was she a goddess, after all, who had come to his aid? Or was he in some strange land of the dead?

"You are a goddess?" The question was barely whispered, and Cal could not keep his impression of her beauty from showing in his eyes.

"Oh, no, no." Now a red blush appeared on Yvaine's cheek. "You don't understand. I was with my father's party the entire time. I even saw your fight with those two men at the inn."

"How . . . why . . ."

"Rest now. I have much sad business to attend to."

"Where am I?"

"You are in my father's . . . I mean, my home, Caltus Talienson. You are my guest, and you are safe here, as safe as any man can be in a world like ours. Now rest. Later we will talk more."

"The sword . . . ," Cal muttered, drifting back to sleep.

The merchant Rafael was not at all the fool he had seemed the night Cal had met him. When not hopelessly drunk, he was a shrewd, practical man who took great pains with his business and family affairs.

Yvaine was his only child, whom he had raised alone from infancy. The girl's mother had died in childbirth, and Rafael had never taken another wife. The merchant's wealth was more than sufficient to provide tutors and maids to teach Yvaine the proper things that a maiden of her station in life should know: dancing, music, and the ways to charm an eligible bachelor into a profitable, secure marriage.

But Rafael, with no son to inherit his business, had needed and prepared his daughter to do much more. She knew mathematics and could study the ledgers of money changers with understanding. She knew cloths and dyes, fabrics, furs, and the tricks of short weights and long measures.

More, she knew men. At least, she knew what her father could teach her of men: how to tell what men wanted, and what they were and were not willing to do to get it.

Often, Yvaine traveled with her father, learning more of his business, providing him with pleasant companionship. But, as always, Rafael was cautious. So it was that when Rafael knew the last leg of his journey back to Dralton would involve passage through an area where bandits were reported active, he had a false bottom installed in his litter as a place for his daughter to hide in case of attack.

Yvaine had already retired for the evening—a matter of wisdom and discretion, as it turned out—the night Cal met Rafael at the inn. When their journey began the next morning, Rafael placed her in the litter without Cal's knowledge, and she had hidden in the secret compartment when the attack began. From there she had observed the whole battle.

"So, the attackers did just appear out of nowhere, as if they suddenly took form from the air itself," Cal said, taking time with Yvaine to relive the events of that dreadful day once again.

"Yes. That is why I do not blame you, Caltus. No amount of diligence could have spotted them. It was as if they were invisible until the moment they struck."

"Of course!" Cal exclaimed, leaping up from his sickbed. "Wizardry! I should have known." Cal began to pace back and forth, pausing to glance out at the bustling city street below the balcony. "I should have known all along. The attack was magical as well as physical."

"Yes, I should think so. Their leader was clearly a man familiar with magic and things of strange gods."

"How so?"

"Did I not tell you before? They were led by a holy man—the same who sat in the inn the night before with you and Father. He did not appear, though, until after you were struck down by that loathsome and strange creature."

"I see. How came I to survive? Why didn't that thing finish me?"

"One guard still lived. When he saw you in the grasp of that creature, he came to your aid. The thing dropped you to the ground, and tore him to pieces."

"Noble fellow," Cal said solemnly. "I don't even know his name. But I owe him a debt that I shall repay to all who are loyal and brave."

"You were left for dead. You were nearly dead, anyway, as I can tell you from nursing your wounds these many days. Our entire party was destroyed. The attackers, including that beast, carried off the pack animals and. . . ." Yvaine fell silent, tears running down her cheek.

"And . . . ," Cal urged gently.

"And the bodies of our dead," Yvaine finished. "Why they did not take you, I do not know. You were left, though they did take your sword."

The runesword! Cal silently formed a thousand curses on all things foul and loathsome. What had become of the sword? How would he get it back? At least, he learned, he still had his armor and his own common long sword. When he was healed, he could fight again.

Cal sat back down on the edge of the bed. Now was no time to be thinking of great quests and magic swords. Now was a time to comfort the lovely woman who had saved his life.

"Good morning, sir."

The serving lackey, Cal noticed, was short of breath, with sweat streaming off his face. The boy seemed sullen, too; he sat the breakfast platter, laden with silver plates, cups, and utensils, on the finely carved table by Cal's bed with loud clatter.

"Anything else?" the boy asked. The way the boy said it, the phrase was more a sarcastic statement than a question.

"Yes, indeed, there is something else," Cal replied, amused by the young boy's attitude. "I would know what it is that makes your face so sour this early in the morning."

"It is not that early, sir."

"No? What is the time?"

"It is midmorning sir. You have slept well and long." The youth managed to make the statement sound like an accusation.

"So I have. But you haven't answered my question," Cal teased.

"It is a . . . private matter, sir."

"Since when do servants have private matters? Especially boys of twelve? Speak, or I'll teach you manners!" Cal roared. His anger was a fraud: it was difficult to keep a stern face when you wanted to laugh so badly, Cal thought.

"Sir . . . I . . . I am learning swordplay."

"Good exercise for a young man. What happened to so depress you?"

"I was bested by my teacher."

"And bested badly, I'll bet. All a part of learning," Cal said, offering sympathetic understanding. "Even the best student is often beaten soundly by his master while learning."

"Yes, sir. Thank you, sir," the boy said, turning to go.

"Wait," Cal ordered. "Who is the sword master here, the one who teaches you?"

The boy's face turned bright red, and tears began to stream down his cheeks. He turned his head, so as not to face Cal.

"Answer me, boy," Cal said firmly, but gently.

"It is the lady, Yvaine," the boy shouted, turning again with rage on his face. "And may your wounds rot until you die!" He ran, disgraced, from the room.

"Oh," Cal said, sinking back down in the bed. "Well, you'll get better," he muttered as an afterthought.

"Indeed he shall, though I will have to teach him better manners." Yvaine's musical voice lilted through the door like morning bird song.

"Yvaine!" Cal said, his face suddenly bright as he sat up again in his bed. "Good morning! I'd no idea you were a fencing master as well as a healer and a merchant."

"A woman in my position must be many things to many people," Yvaine said dryly, crossing to sit in the now-familiar chair by Cal's bedside.

Indeed, she could be all things to all people, Cal thought as he watched her walk. Today she wore a boy's outfit, tight breeches, a short tunic, and boots, and her slender, supple yet strong figure looked even more feminine than it did in flowing gowns.

"You are wise to say that, Yvaine," Cal replied, looking serious. "There are many things a woman in your position must know, and many things that must be done with great care, lest advantage be taken of you."

"Yes, Caltus," she replied, leaning forward in her seat and fixing her wide blue eyes on his, which were so dark, serious, and full of the worldly understanding that afflicts young men.

Yvaine knew what would happen next. It was what she had come for. Caltus would speak now, for a long time, explaining to her the ways of a world she understood far better than he, and she would listen and nod and agree and praise his intelligence and insight and never really hear a word he said and not care if he said anything at all. In time, the talk would turn to his great disgrace, the day the knight for whom he was squire had seemed to run from battle. Cal would curse the unfairness of a world he had never made, and she would tell him he could overcome that unfairness, that a man of his prowess could earn honor again, and more. And then talk would turn to her father, and she would weep, her slight frame quivering with the sobs, and Caltus would take her in his strengthening arms and cradle her face on his bare shoulder, and comfort her, and she would cherish that moment more than her life.

Then, in time, her duties as head of a great household would call her away, and she would return to the world that was real and cold and hard and made athletic swordsmen out of young girls who should have time for love. She knew that one day the realities of that world would take Caltus away, and she steeled herself against him, against that day. For a woman alone in the world could not afford the affliction of a broken heart.

In the days that followed, Cal was able to walk, to eat solid food, finally to take exercise. His healing progressed more rapidly, and his thoughts turned to his missed rendezvous with Bith, Hathor, and Endril. The elf had indicated that there was danger in the offing, danger from the Dark Lord, and that time would be short. Should he try to contact them by messenger? He was not yet healed enough to travel by himself (and, strangely, felt little impatience with this fact). No, he decided, a messenger wouldn't know where to look for the threesome; for by now, they had surely left the rendezvous point. No, better to wait, and in the meantime, heal and help Yvaine adapt to life without her father.

There was certainly plenty Cal could do, he thought. After all, she had a large business and residence to run, and such things required a firm hand. Yvaine was smart and knowledgable, he could see that, but she was so good-natured, it would be easy for the unscrupulous to take advantage of her. He wouldn't be surprised if the servants were stealing her blind already!

A woman in Yvaine's position needed physical protection as well, and that would mean her hired guards should be carefully screened, trained, drilled, taught proper tactics. That was something Cal could certainly do. In fact, he was well enough to begin right now!

"Maid!" Cal shouted. No time like the present to share these ideas with Yvaine, he thought.

"Sir?" The serving girl came rushing to Cal's room. She entered, bowed, and rushed to place clean clothing by Cal's dressing table. Her mistress had left strict orders that his every need was to be attended to.

"Tell your mistress I would see her at once," Cal ordered as the girl busily tidied the room.

"She is meeting, sir, with several men of commerce from our city," the girl said. She arranged Cal's toilet articles on his dressing table and bowed to him again.

"I'm sure she will visit you as soon as her business is done."

"Never mind. I will join her," Cal said grandly. "Go and I will dress."

Cal put on the clothes Yvaine had put at his disposal. Tight breeches, a short tunic of blue with gold trim, a finely worked leather belt, and short boots. Soon, he was sweeping through the large, airy house, seeking his hostess. He passed through room after room, each furnished richly with heavy chairs, tables, and settees, all of finely carved dark wood, many covered with precious fabrics. Servants bustled about on their daily errands, and in the interior courtyard, a small lad tended the fine garden of flowers and shrubs. But there was no sign of Yvaine.

Eventually, Cal reached the main hall near the street entrance to the house, and from there he heard voices from behind closed double mahogany doors.

"And so, my lady, we of the Merchants' Council feel it would be in your best interests, and in the best interests of all the businesses in our city, if you were to consider favorably this honorable proposal of marriage from . . ."

The thin, elegant old man was interrupted by the banging of the doors. In fact, Cal had nearly torn them their hinges in his angry rush into the room.

The sight that greeted him was exactly what he had both feared and expected. Yvaine sat alone at the head of a long table, around which were assembled the leading businessmen of this commercial city. Young and old, they were all of piece: fine clothes, rich furs, fat bellies, soft hands, gemmed rings, and, Cal thought, shifty eyes. Yvaine startled from her seat at the sound of Cal's brash entry; the rest of the company turned and stared in surprise.

"This lady has no need to consider any proposals of marriage," Cal announced, "or of merger, which is what is really on your minds. Now get out of here, you pack of thieves, or my blade will teach you a lesson you won't soon forget!"

"Caltus!" Yvaine barked, sharp reprimand in her tone. Cal didn't catch the undertone, though; he heard what he wanted to hear.

"No, Yvaine, don't thank me, not in the presence of this company. Now, all of you, go! Were you not the guests of this fine lady, my boot would help you find the door!"

"My good gentlemen," Yvaine said loudly and firmly, "I pray you remain seated. This young man has forgotten himself and his place, it would seem, in this household."

"Huh?" Cal said dumbly.

"Good lady, who is this . . . gentleman?" the old man whom Cal had interrupted inquired.

"He is a soldier, hired by my father to protect us in our recent, unfortunate journey. His wounds were severe. I have allowed him to recuperate here."

"It would seem, good maiden," said a youthful banker with cold hazel eyes, "that this hireling presumes upon your hospitality. If his presence distresses you . . ."

"His presence here does indeed distress me. I thank you for your courtesy, Leonardo. However, I am sure that, seeing he has already caused me embarrassment enough, Caltus Talienson will apologize and retire. Will you not, Caltus?"

Cal was stunned. The voice of the goddess was as cold as ice, and there was not even the slightest hint on her face of whatever it was he had seen there during their daily morning talks.

"Yvaine? I am here merely to protect you. Don't you understand, these men are after your wealth, and none of them care about you the way—"

"I have no need of protection in my business affairs, and certainly not the protection of a hired swordsman with no knowledge of such things," Yvaine snapped. "And with no knowledge of manners or proper conduct in society."

"The lady has requested that you retire," Leonardo said, sneering at Cal as he gracefully rose from his seat. "Do be a good fellow and don't cause her further embarrassment."

"Why, you strutting poppinjay!" Cal shouted. "If I'd a sword in my hand—"

"You would no doubt demonstrate that same remarkable prowess that made you the sole survivor of the attack on the late Rafael's traveling party," Leonardo interrupted, flicking a speck of lint from the rich velvet trim on his doublet.

"Villain!" Cal screamed, his face contorting in red rage. "You will answer for that accusation of cowardice!"

"Accusation? I made no accusation, young hothead. I merely remarked upon the great luck that occasionally befalls one such as yourself, one of lower station, who—"

"Leonardo, thank you," Yvaine interrupted. "Steward," she called.

The head servant of the household appeared outside the doors within seconds of her call. Behind him were two armed retainers.

"Caltus Talienson's wounds have healed sufficiently for him to leave. Please help him. And give him a present of money appropriate to his station, in thanks for his services to my family."

"Money?" Cal was outraged beyond measure. "I'll take no money from you, young woman!"

"As you wish. However, I do hope you will reconsider as you leave. There are laws in Dralton, Caltus, pertaining to public nakedness, and you've nothing but my gratitude with which to even clothe yourself. I should hate to think of you in our gaol."

Broad laughter burst from the men around the table.

"If you cannot find the door, these gentlemen will help you," Yvaine said, her gaze cold and hard.

Ten minutes later, as he walked the crowded streets of Dralton, Cal was still trembling with a mixture of anger and shame. One thing was certain; this ridiculous outfit was going back to Yvaine's house, and her money too, just as soon as he could . . . What? Well, just as soon as he could.

CHAPTER
4

Malendor and His Minions

As the last drops of the dwarf's lifeblood trickled over Malendor's tongue, the Lord on Earth of the Undead stared intently into the quivering creature's eyes. There it was . . . the sudden dimming, the descent of the black curtain, the moment of death. The dwarf went completely limp in his grasp. Malendor rose from the great stone throne, his lips still sucking greedily at the dwarf until his tongue confirmed that not even a taste of blood remained in the body. Finally, the black elf raised his face from the curve of the dwarf's neck.

"Refreshing," Malendor said, his words drifting into the darkness above, unheard by living ears.

Then, with a sudden gesture of immense strength, Malendor lifted the dwarf high above his head in both hands and hurled the drained corpse down the three hundred stone steps that approached the great throne. The body bounced and rolled and bounced again and again, coming to rest with a cold thud against the large altar stone far below.

Malendor daintily licked his thin lips with the tip of his narrow tongue.

"Sleep well, dwarf, until I have need of you," he said to the corpse far below, snickering at his own dark humor. "You will not have long to wait."

Not as long as I waited, he thought. For over seven hundred years Malendor had slept the tormented, hungered sleep of the undead, trapped inside the great granite slab with nothing but his own relentless wanting as a companion. Such was the price of failure in the service of the Dark Lord.

Endril, that detestable, loathsome elf! It was all his fault. Once again, as he had countless times in the five years since Bloodseeker had awakened him, Malendor brought the image of Endril's face to sharp focus in his mind. Had it not been for Endril, Malendor would be the greatest of the servants of the Dark Lord, ruling today an empire of the living and the dead—and a number of things in between.

Endril, the traitor, had turned against his own kin, his own blood! Someday, Malendor thought grimly, someday, Endril would pay with torments a hundred times worse than mere imprisonment in a rocky tomb!

How sweet that vengeance would be! Already, Malendor's spies had found the hated, kindred foe. What a strange life he was leading, bound as he was to a group of outcasts such as himself. For to defeat Malendor in the dim past, Endril had performed a deed that ostracized him forever from his own kind. Too bad his loneliness did not cause him more pain! No matter. The pain would come in good time.

But vengeance would have to wait. The Dark Lord had tasks for Malendor, and Malendor was not foolish enough to fail such a master twice. For now, he would have to content himself with keeping close watch on Endril through his network of spies, living and dead, who reported from all the kingdoms and cities of the land.

This time, Malendor thought, seating himself again on the great throne, this time he would not fail. The Dark Elf toyed with a black amulet hung from a chain around his neck as he contemplated recent events and the grand plan for the future. The plan was great in its simplicity.

For decades, the Mistwall had stayed motionless just beyond the Ochre Mountain, near the northernmost borders of the Kingdom of Trondholm, a fair jewel indeed. High mountains guarded the small kingdom on all sides. Among and between those mountains lay valleys fair and fertile, the envy of all who saw them. In the valleys, men had settled, farmers first, then artisans, then merchants. In time, the region grew populous, then prosperous. Its finely crafted items were eagerly sought by traders from the south. Nor were men the only residents of Trondholm. The rockier of the mountains proved havens for small bands of dwarves and gnomes, while elves roamed the wooded lower ranges. As the cities grew, the men who governed them showed unusual wisdom, living at peace with one another and with the scattering of nonhuman races in the land. They even devised a system of self-governing that gave every city, village, and roaming band a voice in the few great decisions that affected all. The orc tribes, while denied a voice in the governance of the land, were tolerated, so long as they stayed within their bounds and behaved themselves.

Not that Trondholmers were soft. No, the mountain valleys were beautiful, but they spawned a hearty breed of men, tough willed, independent, and strong. They would live in peace with any who would deal fairly, but they would tolerate not the slightest hint of servitude. In times past, several armies from the south had tried their hand at the conquest of Trondholm, only to have their forces cut down in mountain pass and valley field by armed farmers and artisans, called out as a kind of militia, under the temporary command of an elected general-king.

This kingdom was the prize the Dark Lord sought. To secure it, he had awakened Malendor. For no being understood better than the dark elf that a powerful kingdom of free men was best conquered not by force, but by fear, corruption, and erosion of the will to good.

What men do not understand, Malendor thought, *they fear. What they fear, they will try to appease. What they*

*try to appease, they will come to worship, if it promises
them something they want. And what do men want more,
than to escape their own pathetic mortality?*

On that simple logic, Malendor based the plan of conquest
that was making Trondholm the Dark Lord's in all but name.
For five years his agents and minions had been abroad in the
land, spreading a vile, deceptive cult. Good men were gulled
by its seeming power and false promise, as they unwittingly,
unknowingly, day by day and deed by deed, lost both their
virtue and their will to life.

It had begun in the small villages. . . .

"I say we go out and hunt this thing down now!" Erik's
meaty, callused fist banged on the crude plank table for
emphasis.

"I agree, friend, I agree," said Henrik. His eyes swept
the table where the leading men of the village of Aarle were
assembled in response to Erik's emergency order. He saw
the hesitation in all their faces and knew the situation called
for delicate handling. "We cannot tolerate child snatchers.
The culprit, or the band, if there be more than one, must
be brought to justice, and your son must be saved. But
we need to know more about whom we're hunting, and
where to look for him. You are greatly upset, and in your
haste for action, you've failed to tell us all we need to
know."

"Then ask Odin One-Eye, for I've told you all I know!"
Erik shouted. He, too, studied the men at the table to see
their response to his rage. In time of battle these men had
rallied to his enraged, shouted commands, for as head man
of the village he was also captain of the fyrd, the village men
assembled as militia. Henrik met Erik's glance with a level
gaze. The four other men around Erik's table stared with
concentration at a point beyond Erik's head, arms folded
across their chests, shoulders hunched down slightly into
their great fur vests, thick curls of dark gray smoke rising
from their large wooden pipes. Their questions remained
unspoken, hanging in the silence like murky gloom.

"It was not a man. It was not a group of men," Erik said at length, sitting down slowly in the chair at the head of the table. "It was a monster of some kind, like nothing I've seen before. It had the shape of a man, yes, but its arms extended to the ground, and it walked with a bent-over, awkward gait. Yet it was stealthy, silent, swift, and deadly. It was in our house, right in this room, before I knew anything was amiss. When I came upon it, it had young Frederick in its foul grasp. I grabbed that axe—there, the one hanging over the fireplace—and hit it with strong blows. Not once, but many times. I could not wound it; I couldn't even knock it down. The thing snarled and seemed to laugh at me. Then it clawed me once with its ghastly dirty nails—the cuts have still not even closed—and then it was gone, racing into the moonless night through the snow."

"You tracked it, then?" one of the men asked thoughtfully.

"Ja, I tracked it. The trail led straight down the valley, away from the village. It was hard to follow in the darkness, and I was slow. But I tracked it until midday the next day, when the trail just disappeared."

"This thing, then, it is a monster," Henrik said. "Some new, strange form of monster."

"The whole thing stinks," observed another of the company. "It stinks of evil, sorcery, and death."

"Not so, friend!" a strange voice called into the room. The entire company startled. Turning, they saw the door to Erik's house thrown wide open. Standing at the threshold was a stranger, dressed strangely. He wore a fine white linen tunic, covered only with a long black cloak of coarse cloth. His gray hair was long and curly, his grizzled beard cropped short. His weathered face wore a smile, and his hard, blue eyes danced with reflections from the firelight. He carried a great staff. A black cloth bag was tied to the simple cord that served him as a belt.

"The strange event that so perplexes you partakes not of evil, nor sorcery, nor death. Indeed, it is a joyous visitation to Aarle, and it breathes goodness, divine power, and life everlasting," the stranger pronounced.

"Who are you, stranger," Erik called, "and how do you know of these events? How come you unbidden to my home?"

"I am called Molchor. I am a priest of the Friends of Eternal Life. Events such as these have been the study of my lifetime, and I come, unbidden, to bring you glad tidings. If, that is, I am welcome?" Molchor remained at the threshold, just outside the door.

"Erik, I do not trust this man. I have never heard of any Friends of Eternal Life. And in time of trouble, the village hardly needs to dabble with the priests of strange gods. I counsel you to let this man go his way." Henrik had risen to his feet, greatly agitated as he made this speech.

Erik stared hard into the unyielding blue eyes of the stranger, taking in his calm, his smile, his quiet strength. The other men sat in silence, awaiting the decision of their leader. It was their village, true, but this was the head man and captain's house. No one's writ ran here but Erik's.

"The night is cold. This man promises information and good tidings. It would be cruel and inhospitable to turn him out without a hearing," Erik decided at last. "Enter in peace, Molchor the priest, and make yourself warm. Then tell us what you know of the evil that has befallen my son."

The old man walked slowly into the room, pausing to close the door fast behind him. "You are wise, head man called Erik, to receive me. I hope you will receive my words also. For those who do receive my words find peace and power in this life, and some find that life never ends." Molchor smiled and nodded to the group of men as he warmed himself by the fire. "Now, friends, sit back in comfort and attend me, and I will answer all your questions."

"Speak quickly, priest," Erik said sharply. "This is a time for action, not long words. My son's life—"

"Be at peace, Erik. Your son is alive, and you shall see him here, in your own house, before this night is over."

"Child snatcher!" cried Henrik, leaping to his feet and starting toward the priest. "Where is the boy? What vile plot is this that you're behind?" Henrik's powerful hands reached out for Molchor's throat.

The priest did not cower; he did not even flinch. His gaze fell square on Henrik's eyes. "Sit, listen, and learn, you overexcited rustic. There are powers afoot here of which you know nothing—though perhaps you need a lesson about them now." Molchor reached out his right hand and placed it firmly on Henrik's shoulder. The angry villager froze in midmotion. His mouth gaped open, the lips trembling. His skin grew visibly paler instant by instant. Then his knees buckled, and he collapsed to the floor.

The other men around the table rose as one, a small host of wordless menace.

"Your friend will be well. He is not harmed . . . though he would have harmed me. Is this your hospitality, to attack the stranger after you have invited him under your roof? Or perhaps you wish to toy with me rather than hear what I have to say." Molchor's calm, steady face confronted the group without fear.

"Speak, then," Erik said. "Say your piece."

"The being who took your son was neither a man nor a monster," Molchor began. "It was an incarnation of the power of eternal life, and it has passed on that gift to your young Frederick."

"You mean it was one of the things that once were called the undead." The speaker, Garik, had held his silence all evening. Now he puffed ferociously on his pipe between his clipped sentences. "Such filthy things were said to inhabit the Bloody Range in ages past." A great blast of smoke rolled upward from Garik's pipe. "Now they are back." Another puff of smoke drifted upward. "The living dead prowl the night in search of human prey. That is what you are saying."

"Yes. The undead have returned to the Bloody Range," Molchor said, his tone indicating more peaceful pleasure than disgust or fear. "They have returned as well to these mountain valleys. They have come now to Aarle. They are, as you say, the living dead. And they do seek humans. But not as prey. No. Your understanding is but partial."

Henrik let out a loud gasp and stirred on the floor at Molchor's feet.

"Ah, there—as I said. Henrik is recovering. Be seated, gentlemen, and hear me out."

At Erik's nod, the men took their seats again, and through the next hours of the cold winter night, Molchor proclaimed to them the new faith of the Friends of Eternal Life.

"In times of old the undead—the zombie, the wight, the ghoul, the vampire, other types not known to you—roamed the earth as its beneficent lords, bestowing upon the loyal creatures who served them the bounties of the Old Gods, gods whose very names have been forgotten by men. They were feared, yes. What mortal does not fear that which never tastes death? We men all fear the immortals, because we do not understand or share their power over our greatest foe, which is death. But in those olden times, men knew, too, that the undead were not to be just feared, but served. Those who served them well could join the ranks of the immortal.

"Then the numbers of men began to swell, and new gods came to serve new wants and new needs. Goddesses of rain and crops, gods of war, feeble divinities to protect cows from the pox and chickens from the rotting of their feathers. Men became trivial, and their gods more trivial still. The old gods, incarnate in the great undead, tired of this world with its petty concerns. In time, they went . . . away. But they did not forget the world of men.

"Now that world is in great danger. A great conflict brews. On one side are a wise few who have rediscovered the glory of the old gods, the glory of human life before the time when a full belly and a contented cow were enough to let a man call himself a man! These few—and I am honored to be counted among the lesser of their growing ranks—perceive that men were not meant to scratch the earth for a few handfuls of grain, nor to root and grub through booths in a marketplace in hope of turning a profit of a few gold coins! These wise ones see that men were meant to be demigods in the service of great powers! Men were meant for glory, power, wealth and honor, second only to the great undead themselves. And for some, immortality is not beyond reach!

"Soon, men of Aarle, you will be called upon to choose sides in this conflict. Will you join the wise, who see man's immortal destiny? Or will you side with those who see you as nothing more than a belly to be stuffed with the seeds of plants?

"The old gods have sent you a sign, a beautiful sign of power and glory. They have graced this house, your house, Erik, in order that you may know the truth and lead your people to true worship and true glory as new Friends of Eternal Life."

The room was deadly still when Molchor finished speaking. Not even the sound of their own breathing disturbed the ears of the assembled men. Molchor's words were deep, troubling, challenging, spellbinding. All gazed at the priest in silence as the fire died down and the room grew cool and dark.

Hesitantly, Erik at length broke the stillness. "You speak well, Molchor, of great things. Do not consider me unfriendly if I must question you more. For what you say is very different from what we are taught by our own holy men, and from what our own parents said. I am not a learned man. I know only that my son is gone. What proof can you offer us that what you say—"

"Proof?" Molchor exclaimed, his blue eyes blazing in the darkness. "Proof you shall have indeed!" The old priest smiled broadly, and his face seemed to radiate a fatherly joy. "You are wise, Erik! Only a fool would stake immortality on a gamble or half-told tale. The wise man seeks proof. I knew I was right to come to you. Here, then, is the proof you seek."

Molchor extended his arm dramatically toward the door, his face abeam with ecstasy. "Frederick!" he cried. "Come in and greet your father!"

The heavy wooden door blew open, inward, as if forced by a tremendous blast of icy wind. On the threshold of the house, framed in the doorway, stood a short, hissing, snarling, wight. Dirt caked its stringy hair, and mud and filth were smeared all over its naked gray skin. Ugly pustules pocked its face, and dried blood stained its pointy teeth. But, despite its deformity, its stooped posture, overlong arms, and guttural voice, every man in the room recognized the human features still preserved in the beast's face.

"Frederick," Erik muttered in an astonished whisper.

"Father," the creature hissed.

"Foul monster!" screamed Garik. The man bolted from his seat to grab the ax hung over the fire behind the place where Molchor stood. "You'll not deceive me, priest, with your strange tales. I know this thing for what it is—a wight. And I know what to do about it."

Molchor only smiled as Garik took the ax in both hands and made his way to the door.

"Die, you demonspawn!" Garik shouted. He brought down the ax in a great blow, directly onto the wight's skull.

"Hnnnhhh," the wight hissed as the weapon glanced harmlessly off its head.

"You cannot harm it, friend," Molchor said. "Though it could harm you, were the god within it not merciful."

"Erik, Erik, it is unclean! I have heard the tales of these things, told by the elves in the high woods. I have heard . . ."

"You have heard the myths of the new gods, who would have you grovel to them for meat and grain," Molchor said, his voice taking on a tone of command. "And you see this being before you through the eyes of trivial men, eyes blinded by centuries of servitude to pettiness."

The priest's hand slipped into the bag at his side as he strode across the room to stand by Garik, facing the wight. From the bag, he took a small handful of sparkling powder, which he sprinkled over the creature.

"Now, behold him as he really is: Frederick, the elected one, Frederick the man, made immortal by the old gods!"

Brilliant light flashed into the darkened room, and for an instant, the men saw before them a beautiful male child, certainly Erik's Frederick, but more glorious than he had ever appeared in life. His human form was perfect, rippling with toned muscles. His skin gleamed, almost golden, dazzling and blinding to behold. The child stood in naked glory, save for a small gold coronet upon his head, set with a handsome, shining jet black stone.

"Father," the vision said. "Join me. Lead our people to immortality, glory, and power!"

From that night, the people of Aarle were Friends of Eternal Life. They did not much like the new faith, at first, and for a while many clung to their traditional gods as well. But in time, all came to participate in the small services required by the immortal gods incarnate. Small services—at first. The great ceremonies, with offerings of human blood from captured victims, did not begin until the third year. . . .

Not all of Malendor's minions and followers were as competent, or as powerful, as Molchor. In places, the cult of death, or the "Friends of Eternal Life" as they called themselves, were resisted by the power of entrenched religions. But throughout Trondholm, in five years' time, there was neither a city nor a village that lacked devotees of the cult.

In fact, progress had been so swift that Malendor, ever ready to curry the Dark Lord's favor, had sent teams of spies, holy men, undead minions, and common cutthroats far beyond Trondholm, to probe the weaknesses of the kingdoms of the south, spreading fear, rumors, and superstition.

Malendor smiled as he contemplated the current state of Trondholm. Ambition, greed, and fear were the common characteristics of the population now. The spirit of cooperation was crumbling. Trondholm's merchants were at each other's throats in trade wars. Farmers withheld food from the hungry to drive up prices. Men everywhere went armed against the growing numbers of thieves. Guided by the holy men of the Friends of Eternal Life, a few even spoke of inviting in the armies of the Dark Lord, to bring order, wealth, and glory to the land.

Soon it will be time, Malendor thought. He closed his eyes and conjured visions of his own triumph. Soon, he would perform the great ritual that would produce a veritable army of undead creatures to pour from Ochre Mountain, into the passes south, into Trondholm itself. Organized resistance would crumble quickly and the kingdom would fall into his palm like a rotten fruit.

But why stop at Trondholm? Already the "Friends" had many followers to the south. It was conceivable that with one great thrust, an army of the living and the dead could sweep the land clear to the southern sea! And behind it, the Mistwall would sweep forward, claiming all for the Dark Lord, and for his greatest servant, Malendor! His name would be shouted from every throat, living and dead! Malendor! Malendor! Live forever, great lord!

Well, thought the black elf with sardonic glee, *I'll do that, anyway. . . .*

"Great one, great one, I bear news for you. . . ."

The urgent voice intruded into Malendor's reverie.

One thin, black eyebrow arched upward as the Lord on Earth of the Undead opened one eye to see what creature dared interrupt his thoughts. It was a human, one of his priests, and a bold one at that. Already the disgusting mortal thing had climbed a small way up the great stairway toward the throne itself! Such impertinence could not go unpunished.

So rapidly the human's eye could not detect the movement, the form of Malendor became a vapor, traveling with the speed of thought down the stone stairs to materialize again only inches from the man's face. The priest did not so much as flinch when Malendor's burning black eyes bored into his.

"You were not given permission to approach me, mortal underling." Malendor's voice conveyed cold hatred.

"I bring news of Endril, great one. News that will be of interest and use to you."

This human thinks quickly, and is not easily frightened, Malendor thought, good qualities for a priest of the Friends when dealing with humans, but not to be tolerated in the presence chamber. . . .

"What is this news?"

"Your enemy stays with the human Elizebith of Morea and a troll at an inn in the far south."

"I know that! Tell me what is new quickly, or it will cost you."

"Great one, here is a sword taken by my raiding parties from Caltus Talienson, another of Endril's human companions. As you see, great one, the sword is powerfully enchanted. . . ."

"Tell me how this weapon was acquired," Malendor ordered. His black eyes were wide with interest as they scanned the blade.

Quickly, the priest related the story of Cal's separation from Endril, Bith, and Hathor. He told of Cal's journey, the fight at the inn with Gunther Stedfyrd, and Cal's employment with the merchant Rafael.

"We attacked them the next day. I planned the attack myself, using much of the magic you taught me, great one."

"Yes, yes . . ."

"We slaughtered the merchant's party and took the sword. But Talienson, I left barely alive. I did not know if you would want him dead, as he is a close friend of the enemy Endril."

"Where is Talienson now?"

"As we speak, he wastes his time in Dralton, mooning, lovesick, over the merchant Rafael's daughter. She nursed him to health in the days after our attack."

"And Endril?"

"He waits with the witch and the troll for Talienson to rejoin them."

Malendor was silent, pensive. Even the priest's insubordination was momentarily forgotten as a complex plan took form in the dark elf's mind.

"Great one? Your orders?"

"You have done well, Garik. Go, refresh yourself and prepare to return to the south. I will have orders for you soon."

CHAPTER
5

Waiting

Elizebith of Morea awoke angry.

At least, she thought she was angry.

Another day, and no Cal, Bith thought. And he wouldn't show up today, either, and that would make him twenty-nine days late. Cal was capable of incredibly stupid and irritating behavior, but this was the worst ever.

Bith's brush snapped through her dark hair with a vigor that suggested she was applying a good beating to her missing companion rather than making her morning toilet.

And where was he, anyway? Drinking in some tavern? Spending days and nights with some four-copper serving wench while she, Hathor, and Endril awaited him with growing anxiety? Had he hired himself out as a mercenary on some fool's errand, fighting someone else's battles while his own went unattended? Or had he gotten himself wounded or even killed in his endless, stupid male pursuit of gore and glory?

Well, according to his own words, there was certainly no beauty here to cause him to come panting back. Bith stared for a moment into the polished reflecting glass. No beauty here, eh? That wasn't what Hathor thought. Then

56

again, Bith wasn't certain that being found beautiful by a troll was a high compliment for a human woman.

But at least Hathor, troll that he was, was reliable! And Cal wasn't.

Or was he? Bith searched her memory, and to her surprise could think of no time since her first association with Cal that he had failed to keep his word, meet a rendezvous, or honor the sacred oath that bound the four together to oppose the evil of the Dark Lord at peril of their lives.

That was the real problem, Bith thought, tossing the brush aside. Cal wasn't irresponsible. He was four weeks late, and that could only mean he was in serious trouble.

Bith remained concerned as she prepared to go downstairs to the inn's main tavern room for breakfast. But now she was irritated at herself.

Many weeks' custom had reserved the corner table near the fireplace in the tavern room for Endril, Bith, and Hathor. It was there that Hathor now sat, munching nut meats. Their flavor was flat, and with a troll's teeth, they were hard to chew properly; little chunks of the nuts kept getting caught in the cracks between the troll's sharp, pointed incisors, which were designed for ripping and tearing meat. These bits were hard to remove, too, for Hathor's sharp, clawlike nails were too large to fit into the tiny cracks.

Nevertheless, the troll was content. He had sworn himself to vegetarianism, and while there were moments when the temptation to taste human flesh was almost unbearable, he had largely kept that oath. Being true to himself gave Hathor a peace that many humans seemed to lack.

Like Cal, Hathor thought, wincing as a sharp slice of nut meat bit into his gum. Cal was so full of anger. Hathor wondered if Cal was simply angry because bad luck had ruined his reputation, or angry because his closest friends were so different from himself, or angry with himself. Whatever, Cal was an angry human. One would have to be angry to enjoy battle so much.

Not that Hathor was shy of battle. "No. I sometimes enjoy a good fight. Battle is not unpleasant," Hathor had once admitted to himself. But somehow, for Hathor, it was different. For Hathor there was no question of glory or honor, no matter to be proved by battle. Battle was what one did when it was necessary. And when it was necessary, one had better do it well.

Now Cal was missing, and that was causing Bith to have no peace with herself. Hathor knew that Cal's words had hurt Bith, even though Bith said they had not hurt her. Bith said she didn't care what Cal thought or said about her. That was another confusing thing about humans in general, Hathor thought. Sometimes they said exactly what they meant. Other times, they said exactly the opposite of what they meant, and Hathor felt that he was expected to know the difference. How could he, when much of the time the humans themselves did not know the difference? Or, even if they did know, changed their mind later on?

Then there was Endril, the elf, who could be even more confusing. Hathor liked Endril. He admired Endril's skill in battle, his courage, his intelligence, his wisdom, his knowledge. All these things were straightforward. They were things anyone could see and understand. But then there was this thing called humor that Endril did. Humans did humor, too, sometimes, but theirs wasn't quite as hard to grasp. Endril's humor seemed to involve saying things that you didn't mean, and that everyone knew you didn't mean, but acting like you did mean it, because underneath what you said there was something that you did mean. This humor confused and irritated Hathor, though he seldom complained. No doubt there were things about troll kind that elves and humans found confusing and irritating, though Hathor could not for the life of him imagine what those might be.

Today, Cal was the problem. Cal was missing. Bith was unhappy because Cal was missing. Endril was, well, Endril was making humor with Bith about Cal being missing, which might or might not mean Endril was worried, too. Hathor was not worried because Cal was missing. If Cal were hurt or dead, eventually Hathor would find the beings who had hurt or killed Cal and exact vengeance. If Cal were not hurt or dead, either he would come to rejoin the threesome, or they would go to find him. Hathor would prefer the latter, but could accept any of the possibilities.

A stubborn piece of nut meat resisted both Hathor's nails and his large tongue, remaining obstinately lodged against his gum, where he could feel its constant pressure. Hathor wondered if nuts were a form of humor created by trees. After all, Endril sometimes talked to trees.

Endril sat with his back to the great oak, his spirit rising with the late-spring sap that carried strength, healing, and new life through the wondrously twisted tangle of branches, shoots, and leaves. The early-morning sun poured its energy into the tree, and peace into Endril's resting mind. Long could Endril linger here, sensing the constant miracle of rebirth and new life, amid the wholesome solidness of life that had come before, been tested, and perservered.

But lingering would not be permitted today. Slowly, reluctantly, the elf released his mind and spirit from communion with the tree and forced his attention to the matters of the day.

The sun was already well up in the sky, its beams chasing away the last of the night's coolness. Hathor would already be finishing his meager breakfast, Endril thought. The troll would be sitting patiently at their table in the inn, waiting for Bith to come down. When Bith appeared for breakfast, Hathor would try his best to allay the foul mood that afflicted the young magician more and more, especially in the mornings. Eventually Hathor's simple, good-natured devotion would charm Elizebith sufficiently that she could be amiable most of the day.

But this would not work for many more days, Endril thought. She was both hurt by Cal, and hurting for him, fearing that some evil had befallen him. How twisted and yet how rich were the emotions of humans! It was as if

the gods, to compensate humans for the shortness of their
frail lives, had given them an intensity of feeling, so that
the emotions that an elf might feel in a century could be
compressed and experienced by them in moments.

Whatever the reason, Bith's feelings were intense and
made even stronger by inactivity. She would not much
longer be content to await Cal's return.

Nor would Endril, for that matter. Cal's delay in joining
them could mean only one of two things: either some great
evil had befallen him, or he had fallen prey to that savage
disease that afflicted humans of his age; the sickness men
called love. The signs had been there before Cal left, Endril
thought. He had seen many young human males in the
hundreds of years of his own life, and always the sickness
began the same way. The first symptoms were restlessness
and a need for action. Next came a general dissatisfaction
with everything, including familiar companions. Young
human males with these symptoms were searching for
love, although they themselves never realized that it was
love they sought.

Sadly, they often did not know which female was to be
their lifelong love, even when they found her. Such was the
cause of the tension that had driven Cal and Bith to say such
bitter things to one another, and about one another. They
could not determine whether or not they were to be life
mates. Endril instinctively doubted that they were proper
for pairing, but with humans, one could never be too sure.
After all, not even the humans could be sure.

Endril judged, too, that Cal was in such a state that he
would think he had found true love when the first female who
seriously attracted him entered his life. Then would be that
terrible time. Endril had seen it so often before. It would be a
time of great emotional sickness, when Cal's mind would be
worth less than a madman's. One day the world would be all
beauty to him; the next he would experience a despair so profound that even elf song would find it hard to describe.

Endril sighed. How terrible it must be to be human, and
yet how profound. How different was human love from elf

love! Human love was conflict and self-absorption mixed with a strange loss of self and great peace; elf love knew only the latter, for it was in tune with the cycles of the earth and of eternity. Elf love had no need to force centuries of feeling into a space of time briefer than a panted breath.

A frown creased Endril's brow. This was no time for philosophical speculation. Whatever had happened to Cal, it was now obvious that the young human was not going to join them here. And they needed him, for valuable time was slipping away. We elves may live for countless centuries and know the calm of a kind of immortality, Endril thought, but we also know that some moments in time are critical in the constant battle between light and darkness, good and evil. That such a moment was coming, Endril could sense as certainly as he sensed the life flowing through the oak behind him.

For in his weeks of communion with these pleasant woods, Endril had felt the bitter chill of the north wind rustling through the budding leaves and greening branches. It was not just the chill of lingering winter, nor the bitterness of the lifeless mounds of ice and snow that capped the northern mountains. There was a chill of evil in that wind. Its bitterness spoke of selfishness, despair, soul loss, and death. And there was something more in the wind, something very old, something very familiar, something Endril had buried in memory long ago and did not want to bring to mind. Yet the dim, unformed memory tugged at him, nagged at him, acting as warning, goad, and challenge.

Very soon, Endril decided, it would be time to search for Cal. Whether the god Vili called them or not, the elf knew that the challenge of evil was coming closer to hand.

"Greetings, good friends! I see the morning sun has already brightened your dispositions," Endril said, entering the tavern room.

He saw exactly what he'd expected. Hathor was trying to make pleasant conversation with Bith, an activity for which the troll was ill suited even if well disposed. Bith was actively torturing a bowl of the inn porridge with a large wooden spoon. Apparently neither the conversation nor the porridge, nor even the activities of stirring, pouring, and dribbling the cooling porridge had done much to improve Bith's mood. The mere fact that the sun was shining was not going to improve her view of the group's situation.

"You're cheery enough," Bith replied sourly. "No doubt the woods were full of comic stories to raise your spirits."

I knew it, Hathor thought. *Trees do have humor.*

"Your porridge will do you more good inside your stomach," Endril countered with a grin. "It makes a poor toy, but is very useful for warming the belly."

"And the heart, as you no doubt wish," Bith replied. She could not keep a faint trace of a smile from her face. "But there is still no news of Cal. How much longer can we wait here for a man—no, a boy—who isn't going to show up?"

"We will wait," said Endril, springing up to sit on the edge of the table, "until it becomes clear to us what else we should do."

"I hope that is soon," Hathor offered, trying to be tactful.

"No doubt it will be, good troll," Endril said. Then, with a nod toward the one other small party in the large room, he asked, "Who are they?"

"Travelers who came late last night," Hathor answered. "They stay to themselves. I do not think they are happy that I am here at the same inn with them."

"Can't have trouble like that, can we," said Endril, a mischievous twinkle in his eye. From somewhere beneath his leather vest, the elf produced a small flute and began to pipe a sprightly air, dancing his way across the room as he played.

The humans at the far table appeared to be a family group. Endril saw an adult male with a female and two young boys. He smiled, dancing around their table.

"Look, Mama, an elf!" the youngest boy exclaimed.

"Quiet, son," the man said gently, placing a warning hand on the boy's arm. "Eat your food in peace."

"Sorry, friend," Endril said, facing the man directly. "I meant no harm. Only a little music to aid the digestion of your breakfast."

"No harm done," the man said pleasantly, but with a guarded tone to his voice. "We are strangers here, and not used to—"

"Not used to elves?" Endril suggested.

"True enough," the man agreed. "At least, not for many months. But we've nothing against elves. There were elves in our homeland, and there humans and elves could work and live together in peace. I meant you no offense."

"None taken," Endril said airily. "Where might your homeland be, where such peace obtains between our races?"

"We are from Trondholm, far to the north."

"Visiting, then, in our southern lands?" Endril probed.

"We come here to live. We hope to find a place for ourselves near Dralton. I have heard there is a need for good craftsmen there."

"That is true. A skilled man, I am told, can do well there for himself and his family. But why leave a peaceful land for an uncertain future?"

"Because there is no peace there now," the man's wife broke in. "Because I'll not raise my children among neighbors who leave nightly offerings for unspeakable things. . . ."

"Wife! That is enough. Friend elf, my wife speaks out of turn. I pray you, go in peace, and let us finish our breakfast."

Endril's face was suddenly grim. "Their offerings are of copper or gold, but never silver, I'll wager. Sometimes of flesh, but never of grain, I'd guess, and always left in fear and hope for a peaceful night."

"You seem to know a lot about these matters, elf," the man said bluntly, a note of challenge in his voice.

"Elves live long. There are few new evils in the world," Endril said. "I leave you in peace, and wish you well."

Endril turned on his heel and strode over to Bith and Hathor. His face was a tight mask as he spoke, and it seemed to Bith and the troll that Endril had suddenly aged, his centuries showing through the grim weariness in his eyes.

"Get your gear," he said briefly. "It is time to look for Cal. We leave within the hour."

CHAPTER
6

Love's Malady

"This city has got to be the mos' miserable city in the mos' miserable lan' in all the earth," Cal declared to the bartender. An unneeded fresh pitcher of ale appeared before the youth, as he had ordered. "Mos' miserable town inna world," he repeated.

"Yeah, friend, it seems you find it so," the bulky bartender said amiably enough.

It was early afternoon, business was slow, and the bartender had come to like this brash young vagabond who had little better to do than spend his few remaining coins in the bartender's establishment. He didn't mind listening to Cal's problems, especially since there was little else to do.

"So, what is it that makes Dralton seem so drab to you? Money or a woman?" the bartender asked. As he spoke, he wiped the inside of a dirty mug relatively clean with the soiled apron that covered his bulging belly.

"All three," Cal replied. "All three. Money, an' a woman, an' . . . There was something elsh, but I can' 'member what 't is."

"Everybody has trouble with women, friend. Why don't you tell me about your money troubles?" It was always good

65

to know a customer's exact standing, in case he asked for credit.

"I can't make no money here," Cal explained eagerly. "I been lookin' for a week or more an' I can't get anything to do."

"I thought you had a job at the stables on the Street of the Clothiers' Guild," the bartender said.

"Did," Cal replied, his head bobbing up and down. "Did have a job there, cleaning the stables. Man there tol' me to go 'way."

"Why?"

"Don' know, don' know. Said I couldn't keep mind on the job, ish wha' he said. I dunno."

"Yeah, 'cause you got your mind on a woman, right, friend?"

"Well, maybe I do an' maybe I don'. No, I don'. I don' think about her no more." Cal leaned forward and eyed the bartender with the air of a man about to impart a weighty confidence. "She didn' treat me very well, ya know?"

"Yeah?" The bartender widened his eyes, as if shocked and interested by this great revelation.

"Yeah. She threw me out. An' all I was doin' was trying to help her. She don' need to marry no mershun's son, does she?"

"I don't know. Does she?"

"No, she don' need to. . . ."

Cal continued on this theme for some time. Eventually, he and the bartender struck an unspoken deal; the bartender stopped listening, and Cal stopped caring whether anyone was listening or not.

Babbling in his cups was the latest in a series of strange behaviors for Cal. Since his unceremonious departure from Yvaine's he had wandered in a stupor worse than drunkenness. Most drunks at least know what it is that they want. Cal had been unable to admit to himself what he wanted, and equally unable to accept the apparent fact that he could not have it.

His first thought after being shown out of Yvaine's was to leave town and travel at once to join Endril, Bith, and Hathor. They were waiting for him; they would be worried by his failure to appear, and they might have need of him.

Strangely, though, Cal had talked himself out of leaving town that day. After all, he still had some obligation to take care of Yvaine, he had reasoned. He owed that much to her dead father. And certainly the girl would come to her senses quickly and send for him. Just to make things easy for her, to make sure her servants could find him, Cal had spent most of that day striding up and down the sun-drenched cobblestone street, keeping a watchful eye on her sprawling house.

He could hardly comprehend her ingratitude when night fell and no messenger had come forth to him. Nevertheless, duty was duty. Cal camped in the street that night until the night watch came along and forced him to either rent accommodations or leave the city. Cal rented a room, determined that in the morning he would make for his rendezvous with his three companions in adventure.

He would have, too, but the way out of town led down that street again, and Cal had thought that perhaps he was being too hasty; perhaps the girl needed more time to realize what was in her own best interests. . . .

And so it had gone on for two weeks. Cal had tossed aside most of Yvaine's gift of money as he left the house. Soon, he was forced to find odd jobs in order to rent space to sleep at night. But he could not sleep at night; he tossed and turned and was tormented with feelings of self-doubt and strange desire. He could keep no job, for aside from being half-dead during the day, his drowsy, frenzied thoughts constantly turned on Yvaine.

Where was she? Was she safe? Had she committed herself to some foolish marriage? How could a person so obstinate, blind, silly, and rude be so beautiful, vulnerable, yet helpful and strong all at the same time? Above all, what did she really think of Cal?

He relived over and over again their conversations, including their last conversation at that horrible meeting. What had he said wrong? Why had she turned on him the way she did? Was there something he didn't understand? Cal wanted to make excuses for her behavior, but couldn't come up with anything convincing.

So it was that Cal now found himself babbling drunk in the middle of the afternoon, pouring out his heartache to a bartender he didn't know, with all thought of duty to his comrades wiped cleanly from his mind.

"Hey, friend, time to hit the road."

Cal awoke to find himself sprawled over a cot that was only moderately dirty. He half opened one eye to see a cockroach on the plain plank floor wiggling its antennas at him inquisitively.

"Come on, friend, time to go. Move it along."

The insistent voice was the bartender's.

"Where . . . ?" Cal began.

"Seems you're in luck. You passed out at the bar in the early evening. Would have landed in the street, too, except that this fellow came around who said he was the steward of the Lady Yvaine, the one who lives in that large house off of the Merchant's Square. He left enough money for you to have this room, and paid me to see that no harm came to you. That was easy enough," the man said, chuckling.

"I . . . I thank you, friend."

"Don't think anything of it. Oh, yeah, I almost forgot. The guy left this letter for you." The burly man pitched a wax-sealed, folded piece of parchment onto Cal's cot.

"Hurry up, now." The bartender closed the door and bounded down a flight of steps.

The sight of the letter brought Cal fully awake. Ignoring the throbbing of his head, he greedily grabbed the parchment, noted the pattern of the seal, broke it, and read:

Caltus Talienson:

I hope this finds you. I would not want our asso-

ciation together to end so unhappily as it seemed to
on the day you left my home. Please be kind enough
to contact me.

                                                    Yvaine

I'll take the upper hand with her right from the start, Cal
thought. He was half running through the city streets, muttering to himself, examining the spots on his dirty clothing
with dismay, and planning his strategy for meeting Yvaine
all at the same time.

*Yes. I'll be firm with her. Tell her there was no excuse
for her treating me the way she did, but, given the grief she
still feels over her father's death . . .* Guilt stabbed through
Cal's brain. *A death that was partly, at least, my fault,* he
thought.

Perhaps it would be better to be completely detached.
"You requested to see me? How may I be of service?" Cal
rehearsed. "Please be brief, as I have many duties requiring
urgent attention."

No . . . that didn't convey the right attitude. What was
the right attitude? How should he feel? How did he feel,
anyway?

"Caltus Talienson? Sir, you are expected at this house,"
a cold voice said behind Cal. The distracted youth turned
to see Yvaine's steward standing in the street behind him.
In his bewildered state of mind, he had trotted right past
his destination.

"Shall I announce you to my lady Yvaine, or will you
do her the kindness of ignoring her summons?" the steward
asked, his icy tone conveying his disdain.

The insult stung. Some of Cal's old self resurfaced, as
it were, by reflex.

"You will announce me, you impertinent varlet, and you
will learn not to pass judgment on the wishes of your lady
if you wish to retain your position."

The older man raised a bushy gray eyebrow. A hint of
a smile cracked his thin lips. "I am glad to see, sir, that
you retain some of your old fire despite your present sorry

condition. Please come in. I will announce you at once."
The steward turned with a grand sweep of his plush blue
cloak and entered the house.

Still angered by the steward's superior attitude, Cal
followed the older man to a room on the second floor
of the house. Though moderate in size, the room appeared
spacious and airy. The late-morning sunlight poured in
through three gracefully arched windows overlooking the
interior courtyard. Rich tapestries adorned three of the
white plaster walls, and a carpet of some exotic foreign
weave covered the center portion of the fine wood floors.
Several finely wrought chairs and setting benches were the
only other furnishings.

Cal paid little mind to his surroundings, though. As he
paced impatiently, his temper rose. Bad enough to be rudely
treated by Yvaine, but to have to endure condescension from
her servants . . . this was really too much! He would just
have to set her straight about . . .

"Caltus. I am so glad to see you again, at last."

The voice of the goddess of his dreams interrupted Cal's
angry thoughts. He turned to see her cross the room behind
him, her golden hair framed in sunlight, her moist eyes
meeting his with a gaze of unspoken adoration.

Cal opened his mouth to speak, but no words came forth.
His palate was suddenly dry, his stomach fluttering in a
terrible way. His right hand raised, seemingly of its own
accord, in some awkward gesture, and he noticed it was
trembling.

Yvaine seemed to glide across the room to take his shaking
hand in both of hers.

"You must forgive what happened that last dreadful day,"
she said softly. "You are a stranger in Dralton, not familiar
with our ways. The men who were here that day were the
leading men of commerce in this city, and in Dralton, commerce rules all else. If I had shown the slightest weakness
before them, they would never have rested until I and my
father's fortune were safely married to one of their number.
As it is, they will probably combine against me in some way,

in hopes that a drop in my business will soften my heart."

"Uh huh," Cal replied.

"I knew you intended only what was best for me, Caltus. But I could not betray my true feelings in front of those men. I could not even contact you as you waited outside the house the rest of that day, for I knew their spies would be everywhere, watching to see if any affection had developed between us. If they thought for a moment that it had, your freedom would be forfeited. These are powerful men, and it is easy to bring charges against a stranger, charges that can take weeks, maybe months, to investigate."

"Affection?" Cal asked.

"Yes, you great, proud, impetuous fool. You know much of fighting, and perhaps something of women, too. But do you know nothing of love?" Yvaine released Cal's hand and lay her fair cheek on his chest, her smooth, clean skin a sharp contrast with his soiled tunic.

Cal's trembling right arm enclosed Yvaine's slight form. The fingers of his right hand gently brushed her cheek, then lifted and turned her chin so that her eyes met his.

"I know little of love," Cal began, his throat suddenly swollen and husky. "All I know of love I have learned from you. I love you."

As their lips touched, Cal felt the most wondrous mixture of excitement and peace he had ever known. Anger, guilt, and self-doubt were swept away. In an instant the entire world became a miracle to be experienced for the first time.

CHAPTER
7

Abduction

All that afternoon, the two lovers explored together the newfound miracle of the world with one another. Caution dicated that they avoid the city's streets, with its wagging tongues and prying eyes. A word from Yvaine to her faithful steward was enough to guarantee the couple the privacy of her courtyard. In the small garden there, the two could find a world's worth of wonders.

They walked hand in hand around and around the same little garden path, talking, laughing, sometimes allowing their lips to lightly brush one another's. Yvaine showed Cal all the marvels of a garden in late spring: the softness of a flower's petals and the delicacy of its veins; the fragility of blades of grass that nevertheless sliced through the heavy, wet soil to reach for the sunlight above; the fine, complex structure of a sparrow's feather that held the secret magic of flight hidden within its near-weightless substance. Everything they found delighted Yvaine. For his part, Cal delighted in her delight, and came to share it.

As the afternoon sun worked its course across the sky, Cal chased the teasing Yvaine around the garden path, glimpsing her laughing eyes through bush and shrub, catching her for a kiss, and letting her go for the sheer joy of catching her again. In time, Yvaine showed her hand as an athlete; she called for her lackey, who brought out to her the little wooden practice swords she used to teach him swordplay. With these, she and Cal fought mock combats, with each other's love as the prize; neither could lose. Cal noticed, though, that Yvaine was no stranger to the use of the practice sword; she was good enough to call forth his own best skill to keep her from embarrassing him with a win!

The sun was just setting when Cal, winded at last, as much from joyful laughter as exertion, threw his weapon to the ground.

"I yield, my lady. Take my surrender," he said, falling on his back to lie in the new grass.

The rose colors of sunset shone through Yvaine's blond hair as she looked down upon the man she loved.

"That I would, my lord, if I could," she said. "Oh, Cal, with an afternoon's dalliance you claim my heart forever, but, my darling, what are we to do?"

"Do?" Cal cried. "What are we to do? Why, that much is clear, as clear as anything has ever been to me. We are to marry, of course . . ." Cal stopped in midsentence, as the overwhelming problems associated with such a marriage fell upon his mind with a crushing weight.

"Cal, to marry me would be your sentence of imprisonment or worse. The merchants and bankers of Dralton will not allow my father's fortune to pass to an outsider, a stranger over whom they could have no control." Yvaine sat on the ground beside her young love, concern for his safety burning from her eyes.

"No, lady, the merchants of Dralton are no problem. I care not one whit for their disdain, their schemes, or their legal plots," Cal told her, his hand resting on her shoulder in a reassuring gesture. "I have been foolish in many things, but I fear no man."

"But, Cal, you don't understand these people. . . ."

"Indeed, not as well as you. Still, they are not the problem. The problem is not one of enemies, but one of honor."

"Cal?"

"I cannot marry you, for I have no position, no knighthood, no lands, no title, no . . . acknowledged honor. I am the former squire of a disgraced knight. For you to marry me now would be to marry shame."

"There is nothing about you I find shameful," Yvaine said firmly.

"You are more gracious than the world. But I cannot marry you until I have proven my honor."

"Then," Yvaine said, turning her eyes to avoid Cal's gaze, "as I said, what are we to do? How long can you linger in Dralton?"

A thousand curses ran at once through Cal's mind. Bith, Hathor, and Endril! Where were they? He had broken his word to them—a fine way to begin to prove his honor! And what quest would be before them? Only the god Vili would know that, if even he knew.

Cal rose to his feet and brushed the spring mud from his breeches. He gazed long into the last light of sunset, until the first star brightened midway above the horizon, high over the roof of the house.

"I must leave with the first light," he said at last. "I have a duty long neglected to perform. These last weeks, I have not been myself, but some person crazed by love's torment. Now that I know your love is truly mine, I must take up again the duty that I am sworn to. Where it will lead me, I do not know."

"May all the gods grant it will lead you back to me," Yvaine whispered into the growing darkness.

"Perhaps it shall," came a raspy, gurgling, answering voice.

Yvaine gasped as she turned her head to see the source of that familiar voice, a voice she had never thought to hear again. A moment later, her shrill scream pierced the early blackness of the night.

Cal whirled about to see Rafael, Yvaine's father, wrap his fat, hideously bloated hands around the young girl's throat and lift her off her feet into the air.

"But right now," the hideous Rafael rasped, "I would have you spend some time with me."

Cal gaped for an instant. The sound of Rafael's voice came partly from his mouth, but partly from the black wound that marked his throat from ear to ear. The merchant's skin was stretched tight and white over his grossly distended body. His cheeks and nose showed signs of rot, and his whole body was covered with the muck and filth of the grave.

"Rafael," Cal shouted stupidly, "you are dead!"

"Father, what . . . ?" Yvaine gasped, struggling to breathe and speak as the cold grip of her dead sire choked off her air.

Rafael did not answer. He turned slowly, still holding Yvaine by the throat, and began to stumble awkwardly toward the house.

Cal hesitated only one moment longer.

"Wizardry!" he shouted. "Wizardry and vile desecration! By the gods, I'll kill you again myself," he cried, hurling himself after the walking corpse. With a flying tackle Cal crashed headfirst into the back of Rafael's knees. His hand reached upward, clutching the mucky, tattered garments of the dead merchant, and with all his might, Cal pulled downward, using both his arm strength and the momentum of his body to drag his foe to the ground.

Rafael's body felt as cold as the water beneath lake ice in winter. The corpse tottered over, falling to the ground with a sickening splat, a strangled gurgle coming from the dead throat.

The fall momentarily loosened the zombie's grip on Yvaine's throat. The woman screamed in terror and pain, as the dead yet living thing lay atop her, its hideous hands scrabbling and pawing in an attempt to regain their hold on her.

Cal scrambled to his feet, grabbed Yvaine's arms, and dragged her from beneath the babbling body.

"It's not your father, not really," Cal said, panting from his exertion. "This is evil sorcery. Don't be deceived! Now run from this house! Run!"

Yvaine ran from the courtyard into the nearest room of the house, seeking to reach the street outside to raise the night watch.

Cal, keeping one eye on the thing he now identified as a zombie or magically animated corpse, frantically scanned the courtyard for a weapon—any weapon. There! About ten yards away, a sundial stood on a marble column about three feet high. Cal sprinted to the column and knocked the sundial to the ground. The corpse of Rafael staggered up to its knees, staring at Cal with cold hatred. The youth stooped, gripped the column in both hands, and raised it into the air. With a scream of rage he charged the corpse as it tried to stagger to its feet. Using all the might of his arms and body, Cal smashed the column down on the zombie's head. The column shattered on the ground. Huge chunks of marble and fine stone dust mingled with the dashed-out brains of the abomination that had once been Rafael. The zombie cried out as its head was crushed, then lay cold and still beneath the broken stone.

"Yvaine!" Cal cried. His lungs ached as they greedily sucked in the cold night air, and his arms trembled from the weight they had just borne. Still, Cal knew he could not stop now. He dashed into the dark house, trying to look everywhere at once for Yvaine. Had she made it to the street? He could not remember hearing her shout to call out the watch. . . .

Cal's foot slipped in something wet and slick on the dark wood floor. He looked up; something dripped from the ceiling onto his face. It was sickeningly warm, thick, and familiar. A trickle of the stuff ran over his lips, and he touched it with his tongue. Blood . . . but whose? He needed light. Why were all the candles out? Where were the servants? And why could he still not hear Yvaine in the street outside, crying for the watch?

Cal stopped, confused. A numbing chill ran through him, as cold as the touch of the zombie in the courtyard. But this cold was from no touch; it was a cold Cal had seldom felt before. It was the paralyzing frost of fear.

A flash of light exploded in Cal's eyes. He raised his arm before his face and turned his head as the blinding light quickly reduced itself to a small point, then resolved into a tiny flame. The flame multiplied, as someone lit several candles in the wall sconces around the room.

"You do not hear the woman because my men already have her," said the tall being who stood with his back to Cal, lighting more candles.

As Cal's vision cleared, he saw that the room looked like a charnel house. Blood streamed from the wheel-shaped chandelier above, where the mangled body of Yvaine's steward lay grotesquely broken. Three hired guards littered the floor, their neatly slit throats pouring forth more gushers of blood to add to the growing pools. And this had all been done, Cal realized, while he and Yvaine were sporting in the garden. The attack had been swift, silent, and deadly.

The tall man lit a final candle, and Cal tried to quickly study him, at the same time fighting down his rising gorge and an unfamiliar sense of sheer panic. The young fighter kept himself from screaming and fleeing only by a supreme effort of will. The man moved with deliberate slowness, giving Cal every opportunity to jump him from behind. Obviously, he was supremely confident. He was a tall, angular fellow. He wore only a plain tunic with a simple cloak. As he turned to face Cal, Cal noticed that he carried no weapon.

No weapon, that is, except his face! A shaggy mane of greasy, tangled black locks fell over the creature's ears and down its neck, and in the front of the face extended down almost to the eyes. But the eyes were riveting: gleaming pools of black-red fire that burned like cinders from the center of the chubby, freshly bloated face. The nose was flat and pug, barely noticeable because the red of the eyes gleamed in the candlelight off the two sharp, fanglike canine teeth that extended over the lower lips. A smear of bright blood stretched across the creature's mouth and chin. The thing flicked its thick but narrow tongue, licking a few gleaming drops from its fangs.

"You are strong willed, young fighter," the creature said. "The others started to flee in terror at the mere sight of me. But you seem content to look death in the face. Then observe how death serves me."

With a frighteningly quick motion, the creature threw itself down on all fours, rather like a dog or wolf, and its obscene tongue lapped blood from one of the pools on the floor.

"Delicious," the creature said, lifting its burning eyes to stare into Cal's face. "Don't you agree?"

The vampire laughed callously as Cal wheeled and ran, ran for his life toward the nearest door.

"Ah, don't leave yet," it said.

It stood, extending one arm in Cal's direction. The door slammed suddenly shut in Cal's face; he ran into it with a bone-crunching thud.

"You are a very rude young man," the creature continued, rising to its full height and striding slowly, arrogantly toward Cal. "For example, you have been quite insulting to your host."

With a nod of its head, the creature indicated the doorway to the courtyard through which Cal had entered the room. Standing there was Rafael's corpse—what was left of it. Cal looked at a standing body with nothing left resembling a face. Black fluids and crushed brains ran down the sides of the smashed skull.

Cal gasped for air. His heart hammered in his chest, and pain shot through his body from his collision with the door. Fear clutched him, flooding his mind with visions of his own doom. He would become a horrid, gibbering zombie, like the brainless Rafael. . . .

Yvaine! The thought shot through Cal's mind like lightning, shocking and cleansing at the same time.

"Yvaine!" he screamed. Strength poured into his legs, and Cal charged at the leering, arrogant fiend with all his strength. He crashed into the thing's chest, at the same time throwing a roundhouse punch at its jaw.

The creature didn't even stagger backward from the impact of Cal's body. The punch hurt Cal's hand. Then a hand that felt more like frozen steel than flesh closed around Cal's throat. The youth felt himself yanked into the air. His feet kicked, seeking a purchase, but there was none. The creature's hellish eyes burned into his own, and the stinking breath of death wafted into Cal's nostrils.

"Is there no end to your impertinence?" the creature asked, mockery in its tone. "Your woman will be mine. Already my men have taken her far from here, while we've been having this . . . chat. Now, as for you . . ."

"Who, or what are you?" Cal gasped, struggling for breath.

"My name is Ulrik," the creature replied, holding Cal by one arm while his left brushed dust from his cloak. "I am, as you have no doubt observed, a vampire, and a very powerful one at that. If I am merciful, I may allow you to become as I am. If not . . ."

"Caltus! Arm yourself!"

The high-pitched voice of a screaming child interrupted the undead creature's speech, and from the corner of his eye Cal saw a tiny, wooden practice sword flying through the air in his direction. The creature, momentarily distracted, turned its head. Cal's right arm reached out and plucked the flying piece of timber from the air. With his left arm, Cal shoved with all his might against the creature's chest, and with his right, plunged the pointed little sword straight through the thing's sternum, burying it deep in the dead flesh.

The creature screamed with such force that the candles shook in their wall sconces. The fiend's grip on Cal released, and it plunged backward, its long-nailed fingers trying desperately to pluck the wooden sword from its breast.

Cal fell to the floor, but was quickly on his feet. He noticed that as the creature fell, Rafael's corpse collapsed in a heap as well.

"Well done, son, well done," he called to Yvaine's young lackey who cared for the little wooden practice swords. "Now, son, find me my real sword!"

"It's here, sir," the boy said, raising Cal's long sword and scabbard in his left hand. "I thought you might have need of it, but I threw you the wrong one."

"No, lad, for this foe you picked the right weapon," Cal said, taking his real sword in hand. "But the wood will only immobilize him. It will take cold steel to finish the job."

Cal stood over the writhing creature, which was still trying vainly to take the wooden sword from its chest. The thing hissed and screamed, kicked and twisted, but could use none of its legendary powers so long as a single splinter remained in its cold, dead heart.

"Now die!" Cal shouted. He raised his sword high and struck a single blow downward with the full edge of the weapon, severing the creature's neck. He kicked the head into a corner.

"To the kitchen, boy, and bring garlic. Stuff it in the thing's mouth. Then await me here. And again, son, well done."

The young boy beamed with pride as he raced off toward the kitchen.

Cal raced out into the street. He searched first in one direction, then the other, but saw nothing but the normal throng on a busy street in a commerical city at night. Then, about one hundred yards from the house, he found a scrap of cloth being trampled by the mindless crowd. He recognized it at once: it was a strip of fabric torn from Yvaine's gown. No doubt she had left it as a sign.

From the direction in which the abductors were traveling, Cal judged they must have passed through the city's north gate. The watchmen there could tell him more. But first, there was much to attend to at Yvaine's house. Rafael's corpse and that of the blood-sucking fiend that seemed to control him must be burned. Provision must be made to safeguard Yvaine's wealth. There would be miscellaneous other duties as well. Above all,

Cal would have to leave word for Endril, Bith, and Hathor. If he was to rescue Yvaine, he would need their help desperately, but he would have no time to seek them out.

CHAPTER
8

Double Pursuit

Hathor stared into the campfire and munched thoughtfully on a large root he'd pulled from a field by the roadside. His own red hair was the most colorful thing in sight except the fire itself. The countryside around and behind him consisted of nothing but rolling hills covered with freshly plowed fields. Hathor had been lucky to find a tasty tuber that had already grown enough to be edible.

Cautiously, the troll glanced from time to time at Bith. He took great care not to stare at Bith. After all, it was Cal's staring at Bith that seemed to be the cause of all this trouble in the first place.

Bith, Hathor noticed, sat staring into the fire, just as Hathor did.

Humans are strange, Hathor thought. It was permissible among them to stare at inanimate things—except, of course, things that humans valued, such as gold, jewels, fine weapons, and whatever else struck their fancy. But it was permissible to stare at a rock or a fire or a tree or a log. You could stare at those things all you wanted to and no one would think anything about it. But if you stared at a human or at something a human valued, there would certainly be trouble.

Trouble was something Hathor and his friends already had enough of. Hathor knew Bith was worried, and that, in turn, worried Hathor. When Bith was worried or upset, there was no way to predict what she might decide to do. She might suddenly decide, for reasons beyond Hathor's imagination, to place herself in the most remarkable dangers. Then Hathor, of course, would have to follow and protect her. Trying to dissuade her with good trollish reasons would be pointless. Once Bith had made up her mind, her will was as unbending as the steel in the blade of Hathor's great axe.

Tonight, for example, Hathor was afraid that Bith might suddenly just get up and . . .

"Don't worry, Hathor," Bith said quietly, pulling her cloak tighter about herself against the night chill. "I'm not going to rush out into the darkness in pursuit of Cal or Endril."

"Hmmph," Hathor grunted. He was always amazed at the way Bith could read his thoughts, even when he took great care to keep them concealed from her. Perhaps she used magic to read his mind. Hathor considered this possibility, then decided she did not. To use magic against his mind without his knowledge would be an unkindness, a kind of violation of his person. Bith would never do such a thing unless it was absolutely necessary for some higher good.

"I do wonder, though," Bith continued, "what it is that Endril knows. He has told me nothing." Her lips pursed in a kind of pout. "Has he confided anything to you that you can tell me?" she asked.

The troll shook his great head sadly. "Endril has said nothing to me."

Bith knew Hathor was telling her the truth, just as she seemed to so often know what he was thinking. Hathor was a good, noble, and simple soul. He would not lie to her.

"Then tell me, Hathor," she continued, her eyes large and serious, "what you yourself think."

How wonderful! Hathor tried hard to keep himself from swelling with pride. That Bith would ask what he thought;

it was a marvelous thing. Hathor realized that ever since his suggestion had been the key to his friends' victory over the Queen of Ice, he had been treated with greater respect by Endril, Bith, and even Cal. But he was still not accustomed to the fact that they honestly valued his thoughts and opinions. Whenever he was asked what he thought, Hathor felt a thrill.

"Well," Hathor responded slowly, "Endril has not been at ease since he talked to the travelers at the inn."

"Yes, good Hathor, that is true," Bith said indulgently. The troll stated the obvious. Endril had exchanged a few words with travelers from the north, and then—boom! He was pushing Bith to near the limits of her endurance, as if finding Cal were suddenly a matter of life and death for the three of them and half the world.

They had come across Cal's trail at an inn three days' ride from their own, a distance they had covered in a day and a half of riding without rest. There they had learned that Cal had been in a bloody fight. No surprise, Bith thought. Further, he had hired himself out to a merchant named Rafael as captain of a caravan guard. Rafael and his party were headed to Dralton, another three days' ride. And now, Bith and Hathor were camped but half a day from that city.

Endril, as was his wont, was out looking for a tree. *Slim chance,* Bith thought, *that the elf will find a forest near here!* For miles in all directions there was nothing to be seen but cleared fields, already sown with the crops that farmers hoped would bring prosperity in the autumn.

"I wonder what it is," Bith tried again, "that those people from the north said to Endril?"

"I do not know. I did not hear what they said, and did not think they would want to speak with me. Endril was in a great hurry after speaking with them."

"Yes, yes, I know. But why? Why is it so urgent to find Cal now, when we waited for him, doing nothing, for almost a full month? What danger has Endril discovered? Why our haste? And if there is danger, what is its nature?

How should we prepare for it? And why won't Endril tell us any of these things?" Bith's questions pelted Hathor like so many hailstones.

"I do not know. Sometimes, elves are as hard for me to understand as . . ." Hathor suddenly stopped speaking. It seemed to him he was about to commit some serious error in human etiquette, though he could not quite understand what that error was.

"I'm just worried, Hathor," Bith said. "I'm worried because . . ."

"Because you aren't getting enough rest. You would do much better to rest than to worry." Endril's voice floated out of the night from somewhere beyond the ring of light cast by the fire.

"Endril!" Bith called sharply. "You should not come up upon us like that. Why, Hathor might have cleaved you in half with that great axe of his."

"If," Endril replied, laughing, "he could find me. Took you by surprise, didn't I, friend troll?" Endril stood up. He was in the grass, not twenty feet beyond the fire. "Hathor," he said, his tone suddenly grave and serious, "your great nose should have scented me long ago. And it would have, if you had been paying heed to guard duty and not to worries. You didn't even see me, and I have been walking toward you across an open field for hundreds of yards. Even human eyes, if alert, could have spotted me as a moving patch of blackness against the dark gray night sky. We are heading into greater danger than you can imagine. We cannot afford to be lax. A mistake like that could cost us our lives, or worse."

"I am sorry," Hathor said. The troll hung his head in shame and looked away from Bith and Endril.

"Fine of you to reprimand him," Bith said, rising to her feet and accosting the elf as he approached the fire. "Hathor has more than proved his loyalty, his courage, and his prowess in battle. And he has the added virtue of not concealing from his friends information they just might need in order to keep themselves alive! It is time, Endril, for you to tell us what you know."

Bith's silver eyes blazed in the firelight. Endril looked at her for a moment, a smile of genuine admiration on his face.

"Very well, Elizebith," he said at last. "I will tell you what I know. What I know is this: the greatest enemy is fear. Fear is the paralyzer. Fear is the killer. If I were to tell you all I suspect, before I am certain of its truth, I would be spreading fear, therefore spreading paralysis, possibly even death. Those things we do not need. What we do need is rest. Had you used this time wisely, to rest, we could be on our way now. You did not, so we will rest until dawn."

Bith shook with anger, but in the end she flopped down on the ground and wrapped herself in her blanket. Endril's will was as strong her own. He had made up his mind to keep his silence for now, and nothing was going to force him to speak.

Hathor, too, sprawled on the cool, damp earth. He still thought Endril looked very old, and Bith very worried.

Dralton offered the threesome a series of vexations from the moment they approached the city's walls. The guardsmen at the gate were firm in their insistence that under no circumstances could anything remotely like a troll, much less an actual troll, enter the city. It wasn't until Endril had piped the guards a lively tune, surreptitiously sprinkled a little dust in the air, and pressed his smiling, charming face practically into their noses that they decided maybe, just this once, an exception could be made. The group's first purchase of the day, an incredibly bulky cloak, enabled them to hide Hathor's appearance from prying eyes on the streets. Still, the troll often found himself waiting patiently outside some building while Bith and Endril spoke with some merchant or city official inside.

At length, the group located the house of Rafael. There they engaged in a singularly unilluminating conversation with a pompous young man appointed by the city elders to be steward and caretaker of Rafael and Yvaine's property until, as one of the city fathers had said to Bith, "this abduction business is resolved."

"And so," the new steward was saying, "Caltus Talienson, as captain of the hired guards of Rafael and Yvaine, has left the city to pursue Yvaine's abductors. Frankly, I think he's a young fool with no chance at all of success." The youth stopped speaking for a moment and eyed Bith appreciatively. He continued with an air of great knowledge. "Everyone knows that kidnappers want only a ransom. If these kidnappers are truly professional, they are probably still here in the city, holding the lady in some hiding place. When she agrees to pay, they will release her. They certainly won't be on some muddy road to the north country, where Talienson apparently has gone."

"I see," said Bith. "You have been most helpful."

"Indeed," said Endril. "And now, if we might just have a bit of a look at the house, we'll be on our way and trouble you no more."

"Oh," said the steward, managing to combine distrust and disdain in movement of his upturned nose, "that's quite out of the question. The council of merchants has entrusted me with the property here, and I hardly have time to give tours. Now, if the lady of your group wished to wait—"

"Here," said Hathor, extending a paw full of gold coins from beneath his concealing cloak. "You take this. We'll look around for a while. Then we'll go."

Bith's eyes popped wide with surprise. Endril fought to keep back his laughter. The steward's mouth gaped at the red-haired paw, but his eyes widened more at the color of the money that paw contained. He took the money.

"Of course, most of the valuables have been removed already for safer keeping, so I suppose you could have a few minutes."

"Thank you, friend," said Endril cheerily.

The man turned on his heel and walked away, leaving the three companions with a moment of privacy to assess the information they had gathered.

"Hathor," Bith said when the man was gone, "I've never seen you do anything like that before!"

"I did it right?"

"You did it perfectly," Endril said with a nod. "Now, what have we learned about Cal? He took a quick job as leader of the guards for Rafael, escorting him here. On the way, the group was attacked. Cal and Rafael's daughter were the sole survivors. She brought Cal here, where he recuperated from his wounds and stayed on, presumably rebuilding a staff of guards. The girl, Yvaine, was kidnapped, probably simply for ransom, and Cal has gone off to find her."

"Seems simple," Hathor offered. "Cal chases kidnappers. We chase Cal."

"Yes, but that's too simple, Hathor," Bith said. "There are a lot of unanswered questions here."

"Like why Cal would have agreed to stay on as head guard here, when his clear duty was to return to join us," Endril said.

"And why he would search for the kidnappers outside the city, when the city officials seem convinced they are hiding somewhere here in the town," Bith added.

"Or," Hathor said with sudden insight, "how a group of bandits could have overcome well-paid guards with Cal as their leader in the first place. The kidnapping would be the second time Cal has lost in combat. That is not usual."

Bith's gaze met Endril's. Endril flushed. Hathor had asked the most obvious question of all. There must be more going on here. . . .

"Let's search this house," Endril said grimly.

The troll went beserk as soon as he entered the court-yard.

"Ooohh!" Hathor howled. "Oohh no, no, no!"

Bith and Endril watched in amazement as Hathor began hopping about, first on one foot, then on the other, shrieking with rage and disgust.

"Cannibals! Cannibals here! Human flesh was roasted here!" Hathor shouted.

"By the gods, he's smelled burnt human flesh," Bith muttered.

Bith was correct. The scent of recently burned human flesh had overpowered Hathor's fine nose as soon as he set foot in the courtyard. The vegetarian troll was flooded with memories, guilt, remorse, desire, disgust, and anger all at the same time.

"Where, Hathor?" Endril shouted.

"Yes, yes, Hathor, be calm," Bith said, trying to stroke the back of the hopping troll. "Be calm and show us from where this smell comes."

"There! There!" Hathor continued his insane dance, but managed to point to a clear spot of ground between several arrangements of shrubs.

Endril knelt on the redbrick garden path. His thin fingers pushed aside the new grass and probed the soft earth near the place Hathor had indicated.

"Yes, certainly, something has been buried here, and the place has been covered over with soil and grass," Endril told Bith.

Hathor could stand the odor of burnt flesh—the odor that in the not too distant past would have been the odor of his own food—no longer. He turned to bolt back into the house and nearly ran over a short human lad who stood in pathway.

"Wait, good troll," the boy said in a low, confidential voice. "You are Hathor, are you not?"

Hathor stopped short. Amazingly, the human child had not turned and run in fear, nor had he made a face of disgust. Hathor knew that his exertions had thrown his cloak aside; the child was clearly seeing him as a troll. Yet he had none of the usual human reactions. He even knew Hathor's name.

"Are you Hathor or not?" the boy asked, moving close to the troll, speaking with great urgency.

"Uh, yes. I am Hathor. Who are you?"

"A friend of Caltus Talienson. And I have a message for you, if you are indeed Hathor, and if those companions of yours are indeed Elizebith of Morea and Endril, the elf."

"We are the persons you name," Bith said, approaching the boy quickly. "What is this about a message? Who are you? How do you have a message for us from Cal?"

"We must be quick. Caltus Talienson told me to trust none but you three, and the city elders have spies everywhere in this house."

The boy, Yvaine's lackey, spoke quickly and quietly. In a few moments, Cal's friends learned that Rafael's party had been assaulted by a group led by a magic-using holy man, and that the "bandits" included some form of hideous thing that either could not be killed, or could be killed only by a magic beyond Cal's knowledge. They learned of Cal's love for Yvaine and of her abduction by beings that, whatever they were, were not professional kidnappers. And they heard for the first time a word that was all too familiar to Endril: vampire.

Cal had ordered the bodies of Rafael and the vampire burned. The boy had obeyed and had helped Cal hide the ashes in the courtyard garden. Cal had then consulted with the city leaders—whom he did not trust at all—and arranged to have a guard placed on Yvaine's property until her return. Finally, Cal had gone north, pursuing what he said was the clear trail of kidnappers, and had left the boy behind to pass word to Hathor, Bith, and Endril, if and when they appeared.

Last, but not of the least importance to that threesome, Cal had left word that he had had, momentarily, a runesword. But that treasure had fallen into the hands of his foes.

All that afternoon and all through the night the threesome rode north, Endril setting a difficult pace. After only a few miles, it became clear to all three that Cal had left them a clear trail, probably hoping that they would be following behind him. Endril followed this trail with single-mindedness, speaking not a word. Not until the horses could go no farther was the elf content to rest. Even then, he allotted Bith little time for sleep.

"Wake up, Bith."

Elizebith opened her eyes to see Endril gently shaking her and smiling into her face. Behind him, in the clear meadow, a campfire blazed, and a pot hung from crossed branches over the fire.

"You can skip the elven charm," she said dryly. "Is it time to eat and move on?"

"Not yet," Endril replied. "Before we proceed, I would point out a few facts."

"It's about time," Bith said sourly.

"Hathor, join us. We are against powerful foes, and you must know what I can teach you of them."

Hathor roused himself and looked with wonderment at the fire, where Endril had a small pot filled with a hot, bubbling, melted metal. Into the pot Endril dipped the blade edges of Hathor's axe. Then he applied some of the molten stuff to his own sword blade. Finally, he plunged several arrows into the mixture, coating the tips.

"What is this metal?" Hathor asked. "It looks like silver."

"That is so," Endril said, "for against certain types of undead creatures only weapons tipped or coated with silver can have any effect."

"Once and for all, Endril, tell us what you know of all this," Bith said. There was more pleading than anger in her voice now.

"I know that Caltus is flying like the wind in pursuit of foes who are beyond his power to defeat, and perhaps beyond ours. From the boy's story, I know it was certainly only luck that Cal was able to destroy the vampire that led the kidnapping of Yvaine." Endril paused to carefully examine the tips of the arrows as he removed them from the molten silver. "Where there is one of these undead things," he said flatly, "you may be assured there will be many more."

For more than an hour Endril unfolded for them his store of knowledge about the undead. He told them of the weaknesses of mere skeletons and zombies, of the frightful powers of wights, of deadly shadow creatures that could not even be seen in any but the purest light. He recounted ancient lore on the incredible powers of the vampire and the only known means to destroy them. He told them the best tactics to use against the undead things.

"Above all else," Endril said slowly and with great emphasis, "never, ever look directly into the eyes of any undead thing. With their mere gaze, vampires can control the minds of mortals and elves. And there are even more powerful undead beings who can take any form they choose. What looks like a clumsy zombie may be something with powers beyond your imagination."

Hathor listened stoically. For his part, he could hope to slay at most a few such things with his great axe, but he could see no way that even he, Bith, Endril, and Cal combined could hope to defeat any large number of these creatures. Still, to a troll, death and defeat were not quite the same thing they were to a human or an elf.

As Bith listened, her eyes squinted and her forehead wrinkled in concentration. She tried to commit to memory everything the elf said. But she could not ignore the rising fear within her. She had the gift of magic and she would use it as best she could. Still, from Endril's description of the powers of these unspeakable beings, she knew that defeating even a single wight would test her limits. She would be no match for a vampire, and Endril indicated there were more powerful things still.

At length, Endril stopped speaking. Hathor rose slowly, took up his axe, and began to gather his meager gear. Endril nodded at Bith, who sat still.

"Perhaps," she said, "Vili will help us."

Without a further word, the elf took the lead of his mount and started up the road to the north. Hathor came to help Bith rise.

"Hathor, is it my imagination only, or does Endril suddenly look . . . older?" Bith asked.

Hathor said nothing.

Moments later, the three companions were pushing their horses again, hot on the obvious trail that Cal had left them.

CHAPTER
9

Heartrune

Yvaine struggled to regain consciousness. Her mind did not know what new horrors it might behold upon awakening, but unconsciously feared that failure to awaken would mean certain death.

At first, she kept her eyes closed. There would be no point in overpowering herself with horrors again. She sought to see what she could learn of her condition through her other senses.

She heard the rats, of course. They rustled and squealed all around her. She could feel the scratching of their little claws as they ran across her bare legs or scrambled up the outside of her gown to sniff her chin. Sometimes, the pain of yanked hair stabbed her scalp as the rats' tiny feet became tangled in her locks.

She felt the cold stone against her back and head and the dampness of the stone. It was very hard stone, perhaps granite, perhaps marble. If it was marble; it was unfinished, for it surface was rough, with protrusions that stuck painfully into her back.

She felt the cold iron bracelets on her wrists, and when she moved her arms, she heard the clink of chains.

So, she decided, *I am lying chained to a cold slab of rock, probably in a some dungeon. The place is damp and full of rats. It is probably very dark, and it may even be safe to open my eyes now.*

Still she hesitated, for it was the sight of horrors she dreaded most. In her mind she could not erase the horrid image of her father's walking, gibbering body, grabbing her, trying to carry her off. Nor had that been the end of her nightmare, though it was the worst. She had been grabbed by vile men who were more beastlike than human. They had beaten and manhandled her. She had been stuffed, half-conscious, into a large cloth sack like so many pounds of vegetables. She had been able to tell, from the jostling she received and the sounds of hoofbeats, that she was being taken out of the city on the back of a horse.

Then she had met the holy man, the priest, Garik, the same one who had directed the attack that killed her father. He awaited her in the dark night astride a great flying beast that looked like the dragons in the tapestries of her home. Whether the thing was a dragon or not, she didn't know. It was a huge blackish green thing, with leathery wings. She had been forced into a kind of saddle on this creature's back. Garik, too, had mounted the beast. Then at Garik's command the creature had risen into the air. The great wings, easily thirty, perhaps even forty feet across, had beaten faster and faster and faster. With unbelievable speed, the thing had whisked her through the black night sky.

How long that ride had taken she could not tell, for she had finally fallen unconscious along the way. And now she was here—wherever this place was.

Yvaine opened her eyes. Her scream wasn't even heard, for it could not penetrate the solid rock walls of her little cell, and the only ears that would have cared to listen were far away, down miles of corridors carved far beneath the Ochre Mountain.

•   •   •

"Well, Garik?"

"All is as you ordered, Great One. Talienson is alive. Even now he pursues those he believes to be the abductors of his beloved."

"And the girl?"

"She is here. I brought her myself. The wyvern you gave me made great speed, as you promised."

"And Endril?"

"At last report, our spies saw Endril with the troll and the witch leaving Dralton, following Talienson's trail."

"Perfect. Garik, you have done well. Very soon, Garik, very soon, you may join the ranks of the immortals. And I will have a special task for you."

"I live only to serve you, Great One."

"Naturally. Now go."

Malendor watched as this human priest scuttled away into the darkness below the great throne. The black elf congratulated himself for being lenient with Garik's earlier impertinence. Humans must be ruled with terror, certainly, but terror mixed with occasional kindness could produce exceptional results, like Garik. There went a true believer; a man so thoroughly corrupted he believed in the righteousness of his cause and looked forward to his reward.

With wise handling of humans like Garik, Malendor would soon have success beyond even the Dark Lord's imagination. He would have Trondholm, he would have Endril, and he would have countless kingdoms to the south. The Mistwall would move farther in six months' time thanks to Malendor than it had moved altogether in the past . . . how many years?

But first, there were more preparations to be made. The girl—what a perfect prize! Of course, she could serve his purposes living or dead. It mattered little whether she became a willing follower of his cult or a midnight snack of virgin blood. Still, his triumph over Endril would be more perfect, more complete, if the girl could be turned to evil of her own free will. . . .

• • •

By the sputtering light of the single torch in her cell, Yvaine saw the mist forming in the center of the room. She felt terror rise in her again, but her body and mind were too numb to experience it fully. It had taken hours for her to control her reaction to the sight and smell of the rotting corpses that littered the room. Once, it appeared, they had been neatly stacked, like cordwood. But rummaging hands had toppled the stacks, and now corpses in all states of decomposition were strewn about the floor.

The mist, at least, was something different to look at, even though it seemed to emanate pure evil.

In a moment the mist resolved itself in a form. Not a human form, but a form something like that of a man. Perhaps, Yvaine thought, an elf, but unlike any of the few elves she had ever seen. This being was taller than a normal elf and had none of the natural goodness that seemed to come from elven folk, even when they were of a mischievous mood.

Yvaine summoned her courage to speak. If she was to survive, it seemed important to try to seize the upper hand, just as in negotiations with Dralton merchants.

"What are you?" she asked.

The sudden question so shocked Malendor that he stepped backward, stunned. The bruised, beaten, chained woman before him should have recoiled in terror at his mere presence. Instead, she greeted him with an interrogation! And Malendor was forced to admit to himself that her question was possibly the one question he could not answer.

How many centuries ago had he given his life force to the Dark Lord? How many rituals had he performed? How many had he suffered to be performed on him, to make him into what he now was? He was a being possessed of all the power of all the forms of the undead. He could become any of them at will. He could summon them, control, send them to do his bidding without fear that even the most powerful would dare disobey him. He could live, perhaps forever, without feeding, though the hunger of the vampire would torment him. But what was he? In his innermost self, Malendor was forced to confess that he did not any longer know the answer to that one question. Malendor's hand reached up to rub the black stone amulet that hung from his neck. He stared at Yvaine with ill-concealed hatred.

"Silence, mortal!"

Malendor's roaring voice of command echoed off the walls of the small room, so loud and yet so low pitched that Yvaine could feel the vibrations in the stone beneath her. The countless rats in the room squealed in terror and began to disappear to wherever frightened rats can hide.

"You are not here to question me," the shaken Lord on Earth of the Undead stated. "You are here to obey."

What a creature she was! She had caused him to lose his composure, and look! She knew it! Malendor could see it in her clear blue eyes; the look of a human who knew it had scored against a powerful foe. No matter. He was in control of himself again. Her strength would make her seduction to his will that much sweeter.

"How powerful you are!" Yvaine said, straining to raise her head. "You have the power to attempt to intimidate a captive woman. I am greatly impressed." If only she could keep this thing off balance, buy time. Perhaps by some miracle, Cal would come. . . .

For a moment, Malendor considered simply meeting her gaze. Her will would be his within an instant; she could never resist the power of his magic. But that was not what he had planned. He would abide her taunting for the time being.

"Lady, I confess I am quite undone by you," Malendor said, smiling sweetly. "Most humans react to my presence with terror and hatred. Forgive me if my usual response to such reactions was automatic. I see that you are quite a superior individual."

"Do you always keep those you consider superior chained in a charnel house?"

"Do you object to the presence of death?"

"I object to abduction, murder, desecration of the dead, and many other vices, such as arrogance, all of which I see around me."

"Ah," Malendor replied. He strode toward her with a look of genuine concern on his face. "But what if those things you call 'abduction' and 'murder' are really liberation? What if what you call arrogance is the natural celebration of the true fullness of life? In short, what if you have been deceived by the teachings of others who lack your capabilities?"

"I don't understand. Nor do I care to. I am certainly capable of judging good and evil for myself, and what I see here is vile, disgusting evil," Yvaine retorted. She wondered how much longer she could keep bantering with this terrifying creature.

"I agree with you," Malendor said calmly. He seated himself on the stone slab that served as Yvaine's bed and prison. "Death is evil."

Yvaine looked at the creature who was now so near she could feel the coolness of his body. He simply smiled, avoiding her direct gaze, and waited for a reply.

"Well, yes," Yvaine said at length, out of the seeming necessity to say something. "Death is evil."

"That is why," Malendor continued quietly, "I seek to give life."

Yvaine could stand no more. Her mind would no longer function, and her emotions, though numb, could still register anger.

"Is this what you call giving life?" Yvaine was screaming now, almost hysterical. "Look at these corpses! What respect for life does it show to leave the dead to rot in a stone room, unburied, unmourned, uncared for?"

"To answer your first question, I do not call this giving life. Calm yourself and observe, and I will show you what I mean by 'giving life.' "

Malendor rose slowly. He stretched out his right arm, his palm upward, his long, narrow fingers extended toward the center of the pile of corpses.

"Rise!" he commanded. His arm swept upward in a dramatic gesture.

Yvaine watched, stunned to speechlessness, as slowly, the dead began to twitch, then to move their limbs, then to disentangle themselves from one another. Gradually, the lumbering forms gained their feet. Some took a few feeble steps; others simply stood, their dead eyes rolling about to take in their surroundings.

"You see, death is an evil I can overcome. It is tragic that fear prevents many from hearing my message."

Malendor swept grandly from the room. The horde of zombies followed.

He visited her once per day, taking care to bring her wholesome food and, on each occasion, some new comfort. Water for washing first; then a pallet to lie upon; then clean garments; then books—particularly the holy books of the various religions practiced in her home of Dralton. With each visit, he renewed the discussion of his message of overcoming the evil of death with eternal life.

"But, but, you merely animate the dead. They do not truly live," Yvaine objected one day.

"Ah, mere animation of corpses is but the first step toward the giving of life. For some, it is sadly true, that is the most that I can do. But among those you call the living, do not some live more fully than others? Were there in Dralton no defectives, no idiots, no blind, no lame, no halt? Were there none there who could never experience the fullness of life that you yourself came to know?"

"Of course there were, but—"

"Why should you expect an equality in eternal life when there is none in the first life?"

"Well, I, I, I don't know. I simply thought—"

"There is an order in things, is there not? Some are stronger, some are weaker. Some are powerful, some are not. Some live fully, some do not. Some are superior, as you are. Many, alas, are not."

"What do you mean, as I am?"

"I knew from the first that you had the potential to truly experience immortality to the fullest. Did I not tell you when we first met that you were a superior being?"

"Yes, you did."

"You could be great among those who live forever. Imagine the good you could do, if you had even a portion of the power I enjoy. That can be yours, if you want it."

"How so?"

"The process is quite simple."

"What would it involve?" The notion of power intrigued Yvaine. Now that her health and her mind were partially recovered, she realized that obtaining part of this creature's power could be the key to her own survival at his hands. And, also, she often thought of the things he said, and they seemed, oddly, to make a kind of sense to her.

"The first step is really nothing, although you would sense quickly the flowing of newfound power, immortal power, into yourself."

"What is that step?"

"We merely share a tiny bit of one another's blood," Malendor said offhandedly.

"But then I would be . . ."

"Oh no. You would only begin the process of transformation to your immortal form. The final change takes many such steps. But to begin your transformation would let you experience, as it were, a taste of immortality. . . ."

The day came when Malendor triumphed. Seduced by his subtle arguments, driven by her desire to have power—any kind of power—in a situation in which she was otherwise powerless, Yvaine drank from the cup that Malendor offered. From that moment, her soul was his, and she descended inexorably down the path of vampirism.

On that day, Malendor took from Yvaine, with her consent, a lock of her hair. With it, he performed in the privacy of his study a secret ritual. That night, the wyvern, again hastened beyond all imaginable speed by Malendor's spells, once more took to the air.

CHAPTER
10

Battle on the Moor

Cal was frustrated nearly to despair. At first, the trail of the abductors had been easy enough to follow. There were fresh tracks on the muddy road, and for several days Cal could find those tracks by midmorning, indicating he was a day or less behind his quarry.

After three days, though, the trail led off the road into the rough. Not that the terrain was difficult; plowed fields were easy to negotiate, and the kidnappers were easier still to track in damp soil.

Then came three days when Cal needed more than six hours to find their trail. When he did, it always seemed to double back in some direction he had already come. Never did the trail lead back to exactly the same locations, but always it doubled around. At the end of six days, Cal was certain he was traveling in circles.

On the seventh day, the trail disappeared completely. Cal worked his way outward from his campsite of the night before, tracing wider and wider concentric circles, looking for any sign of the kidnapper's passage. He could find none. By late afternoon, he was back to the main highway north—and there he found the trail again.

He rode hard, and by late night estimated he was only a few hours behind his foes. But his frustration was gnawing away at him.

What if, on the morrow, the trail was impossible to find again? What if the kidnappers doubled back again? What if they traveled all night, realizing he was close behind them? Clearly they knew something of his movements; how else could he explain their tormenting route? It was almost as though they were teasing him, taunting him, torturing him.

And torture it was. For his other constant thoughts were of Yvaine. What manner of hideous creature had her in its clutches? The thing at the house had certainly been a vampire, and it had probably been the power that animated the corpse of poor Rafael. That vile beast had said its "men" had taken Yvaine . . . but could Cal believe the word of a vampire? Hardly.

Would he be in time? What harm would be done to her? Would her gentle goodness be so shocked by confrontation with so horrid an evil that her mind would be unhinged? These, and thoughts of even worse fates for Yvaine, were a constant torment to Cal.

A swollen, bloated, orange full moon rode high in the sky when Cal finally reined his horse to a halt. The reliable animal badly needed rest, and no matter how strong Cal's will, it could not overcome that demand that nature made upon the poor beast. The young fighter tended to his mount, then strode to a nearby hill to survey the countryside under the murky moonlight.

It was strange country he had come to in his pursuit. The ground was not gently rolling, as were the hills near Dralton. Instead, there were large, flat plains, punctuated by hills and mounds that seemed to suddenly erupt from the landscape as if the earth had been hit from the underside by the fist of a god.

Nor was the land here cleared. There were no fields and no crops. Instead, a kind of tawny, long, thick grass grew in tangled patches. Between those patches rose a few varieties of scrub brush and, occasionally, a few stunted trees. From the sides of the hills great stones projected upward at wild angles, making strange shapes against the cloudy, moonlit sky.

Moors, the few local folk called these lands.

Here and there Cal saw stones piled on one another in what seemed to be some purposeful way, but what the purpose was or might have been he could not guess. And whether the hands that had piled them were human was an open question as well.

There were few signs of animal life, and Cal was forced to take food from his meager provisions. Still, he thought, there must be some game to hunt in this wild land, for the howls of distant wolves cut through the night silence, rising to greet the moon on her endless course.

Not many miles away, Endril too stood atop a hill and gazed out upon that same land. His slender figure was framed in the pale moonlight against the night sky, but no eye beheld him. Behind the elf, at the foot of the broken, rocky slope, Bith slept soundly, rolled in her blanket and cloak. The horses were tethered not far from the sleeping sorceress. There was no fire this night; Endril had thought it unwise. Near Bith's sleeping form, Hathor sat on a large, flat rock, his axe resting across his knees. As always, the troll kept his constant watch, but his eyes were not upon Endril.

The elf took time to look over the twisted, bizarre landscape, feeling a strange peace as night fog drifted by in wisps and patches.

How much there was to see! The elf's memories blended with his current vision; he saw into the past. He saw the hunting parties of men dressed crudely in animal skins and furs trudging along familiar paths through the forbidding dark land. Their gutted kills they carried tied to long poles supported on their shoulders. In their hands they carried heavy clubs, crude spears, and axes with great stone heads. Even in the darkness, he could see the swirls of wode on their arms and faces, the blue paint applied in patterns carefully calculated to inspire terror in any human foe.

Tonight, the moon was full. These savage men would feast late in their strange man-made caves. Then, before the fat orb had settled to the horizon, they would rise and go to their huge stone altars, where they would offer a living sacrifice to the great lady of the night sky. There would be blood and terror, yes, but also a kind of peace, a harmony with the patterns of nature, that Endril could not help but admire.

Endril shook his head to clear his mind. That had been long ago, hundreds of years ago, when men were more openly savage but much simpler. Now the landscape before him was deserted, save for Cal, who was out there somewhere, and those Cal pursued. The only things astir on the moors, Endril mused, were creatures caught up by the gods in the endless struggle between good and evil. Ironically, throughout time, both sides had claimed the moon as their ally. The powers of evil valued her for the darkness that surrounded her; the powers of good celebrated her for her light.

Soon, very soon, Endril thought, there would be a small skirmish in that never-ending battle. Cal's trail in the last three days had become an erratic combination of zigzags and circles. If the kidnappers Cal followed were truly headed for a country far north, why did they amble back and forth in this barren country? Perhaps they awaited something. Perhaps they had some more sinister plan afoot. In any event, a collision would take place soon. Endril knew his own group was not far behind Cal, and the signs of Cal's renewed haste hinted that Cal was not far from his quarry.

It was time to prepare for battle. The elf walked down the rocky slope of the hill to the darkened campsite. With a nod to the great troll, Hathor, he began to carefully check his quivers of silver-tipped arrows.

Bith lay still and peered into the night. She saw Hathor sitting at guard over her and felt more secure as she pulled her blanket tighter around herself. Through the weedy grass that was all that grew on this endless moor, she saw Endril carefully checking the tips of his arrows.

They think I am asleep. Let them think that. Endril will simply tell me to go back to sleep if he knows that I'm awake, Bith thought.

Tonight, Endril had stayed near the camp, and now he had rejoined it, long before dawn. Bith knew what that meant. They were close to Cal, close to the kidnappers, and very close to danger.

Bith tried to understand what had possessed Cal to undertake this rescue mission by himself. Why hadn't he come for them first? Was he so smitten by this merchant's daughter that he had lost all reason?

Quietly, so Endril and Hathor would not hear, Bith rubbed a small piece of reflective metal on her blanket, polishing its surface. Then, when the moonlight shone full through the drifting clouds, she gazed into it. She could just make out her own form: the flowing hair, the strangely silvered eyes, the high cheekbones, and the lips that seemed both full and thin at the same time. No beauty? Perhaps not, Caltus Talienson. Perhaps not. But there is loyalty in this face.

Even as she stared into the cool metal, the face seemed to change. At first, Bith thought the moonlight was playing tricks on her eyes, but as she watched, she saw her refelction gradually replaced by a male face, a bearded face, the face of one with great authority. . . .

Vili!

About time, Bith thought. *No doubt he'll demand the usual obeisance.*

The familiar voice of the god sounded quietly in her mind.

"Remember well these words, Elizebith of Morea," it began. It spoke quickly, urgently, for some time. And not once did it demand the usual tokens of worship and respect.

Cal was riding, riding as hard as he could, pushing his poor horse beyond her limits. The barren plain stretched endlessly before him. On the far horizon he barely could see a black steed bearing a rider who wore a large, flapping cloak the color of dried blood.

On and on Cal rode, digging his heels into the flanks of his mount. Ahead, the rider in the dark cloak stopped. He turned to see Cal slowly closing the distance between them.

"Hyah! Hyah!" Cal cried, trying to gain yet more speed. A few moments more, and he could see the burden the rider carried. Yvaine! She was dumped over the back of the black stallion like a corpse.

The rider stood his ground, waiting. Finally, Cal could see his face. It was a cold, white, cruel, leering face. The man began to laugh as Cal drew closer still. His cackling cracked the cool air and sent a chill through Cal.

Almost there—almost there! Cal drew his sword and leaned forward even further, a warrior at the charge.

Then, seemingly from nowhere, scaly, mud-covered arms reached up out of the earth itself, grabbing at his horse's feet. His mount stumbled, then reared in panic. Cal tumbled off backward.

Undaunted, he leaped to his feet and ran on foot toward the grinning foe. Yet again, arms and hands reached out of the earth, hitting his shins, clutching at his ankles, clawing at his legs, hindering him, then stopping him. He was only two swords' lengths from the laughing fiend, only three steps from his beloved Yvaine, but he could go no farther. Inexorably, the clutching hands dragged him down, down, down, as if the earth itself would slowly swallow him.

"Caltus!" called a deep booming voice.

"Not now, not now! Must save Yvaine . . ."

"Caltus!" the voice demanded.

"Go away. Must save Yvaine, must save . . ."

Cal awoke screaming Yvaine's name. He sat bolt upright, gasping, trembling in the cold. Anxiously he looked around at the empty landscape, as if to assure himself that he had, in fact, been dreaming.

Three times that night Cal's dream returned. Three times the voice called to him. Three times he refused to answer the strange voice, his every thought upon Yvaine. And three times he awoke from the nightmare. Each time, his confidence was shaken a little more.

No point trying to sleep, Cal decided after the third occurrence of his frustrating, terrifying dream. The first faint light of dawn was trying to break on the moors. The highway stretched before him. Cal roused his half-rested mount, saddled up, and rode ahead, following the still-clear prints of those he had come to think of as his prey.

"Endril! Hathor!" Bith emerged suddenly from what her two companions had mistaken for sound sleep, jumped to her feet, and was already heading toward her mount as she spoke.

"We've no time to lose," the enchantress snapped. "Cal is moving again, and he is only a short distance ahead of us. The trail we're following doubles back to the highway. We can catch up to him if we cut across country, but we must move now!"

"I thought as much," Endril replied calmly, gathering his gear.

Hathor, too, rose, axe in hand. That was sufficient preparation for him. But one thing puzzled the troll.

"How do you know where we can find Cal?" Hathor asked.

"Vili. He came to me in a dream," Bith replied. As she spoke, she searched the ground around her. In a moment's time she found a medium-size branch extending from one of the small, scrubby trees that grew in the area.

"Hathor, if you please, cut and trim this branch for me. Quickly."

Hathor did as Bith commanded. She was mounted and ready to ride when he handed her the crudely fashioned staff. No sooner was it in her hands than she started away at a trot.

"Bith! Wait!" Endril's tone, too, was commanding. "What did the god tell you?"

"He told me how we might find Cal."

"And what else?"

"The words to an enchantment that may save all our lives."

Endril nodded slowly. "Shall we now call you a priestess?" he asked. His tone was serious, not teasing.

"Call me what you will," Bith replied. "But we must hurry."

"Then we ride," Endril declared. "Come, Hathor! I will take the lead. You follow Bith, and watch our rear well. And, Hathor, it may be that your nose will be of more value than your eyes!"

A moment later, the three were crossing the broken moors at a canter. Jagged stones jutted out of the ground, half-hidden in the tall, tough grass. There were countless places for man or horse to trip and fall. The group's pace would have been reckless, if not impossible, had all been humans, but Endril's sharp eye picked out the countless pitfalls in the broken ground, even in the predawn light.

Twice they came upon groups of large mounds jutting out of the earth.

"Straight ahead!" Bith called to Endril.

But both times the elf turned, riding wide of the mounds by as much as half a mile. He had to slow his pace as he did so, for his attention was divided. Bith noticed that he continued to watch carefully the path ahead, but closely observed the mounds as well. Why Endril did this she could not guess, but she did not question his actions.

By the time the sun's full orb was visible above the jagged horizon, Endril could see the track of the highway cutting across the moor between two groups of low hills. He reined to a halt.

"Elizebith! There's the highway. Cal must be very near—but these hills are blocking the view." The elf raised one eyebrow, and a suggestion twinkled in his eye.

Bith and Hathor halted next to Endril, and Bith quickly dismounted. She stood quite still, and for moment appeared to be in a mild trance. Her hands made a few small gestures, and she muttered in a tongue completely alien to Hathor, though partially understood by Endril.

"What is she doing? Is she making magic?" Hathor asked.

"*Shhh,*" answered the elf. Then he whispered, "Remember, never break her concentration when she is reciting a spell."

"Oh," Hathor said, nodding.

The troll watched in awe, the elf in mild admiration, as Bith began to float slowly upward in the air.

"She has worked on this quite a bit," Endril confided to the troll. "The basic spell is not difficult, but control while one is levitating can be tricky."

Hathor nodded dumbly. He was accustomed to seeing magic performed, and had even been levitated by Bith himself, but was still awed by magical power. When Bith performed magic, Hathor's admiration for her was doubled.

Bith floated higher and higher, scanning the landscape ahead.

"Your control is much improved," Endril shouted up to her. Though the compliment was sincere, it carried a not-too-subtle reminder of the several times she had bumped all of them into high tree limbs while practicing this particular spell.

"Hmmph!" Bith grunted back. "Just because magic seems to come naturally to your race, you think we humans—"

"Bith! Danger!" Hathor's booming shout interrupted the banter.

Endril wheeled around and saw the troll pointing with his axe to a spot high in the air behind Bith. There, swooping down upon her, was a huge dragonlike being. It was greenish black in color, with scaly skin, leathery wings a full thirty-five feet across, and a huge tail that ended with a stinging weapon fully the length of a long sword.

"Bith! Get down!" Endril shouted. The elf silently cursed himself; in order to be sure his bowstrings stayed dry, he had not yet strung his bow! "Hathor—my bow is not ready," he said as calmly as he could to his mighty companion.

But Hathor was already in action. The troll held his axe in both hands at full arm's length in front of his body, and spun himself around and around, faster and faster. Bith, seeing her danger, was descending as quickly as her control of her spell would allow. The oncoming attacker continued its dive, coming lower and lower until . . .

"Yaaah!" Hathor screamed, letting the axe fly. The deadly missile leaped from his hands and hurtled skyward with blinding speed. The diving wyvern had no chance to alter its course before the axe struck it squarely in its soft, poorly armored underbelly. The great weapon buried itself in the wyvern's flesh so deeply that only a portion of the haft remained visible.

The flying creature let out a scream of pain and rage as its wings beat the air. It leveled off, lost speed, and tried to gain altitude. Bith continued her descent, and the creature streaked upward over her, blackish blood and gore dripping from its huge wound. By the time Bith's feet touched the ground, Endril's bow was strung and ready, and the skilled elf let fly two quick shafts in pursuit of the retreating beast. The first struck the monster near the midpoint of its tail; the second fell short, so great was the creature's speed.

The huge Hathor gripped Bith's shoulders tightly, as if to hold her on the ground even while attempting to comfort her.

"Are you hurt?" Hathor asked. Now that the danger was past, a trace of panic sounded in the troll's guttural voice.

"No, Hathor," Bith said, "I am unharmed, thanks to your keen eye and great strength."

"Bith, I owe you an apology. I should have kept better watch while you—"

"There is neither time nor need for apologies, Endril. Cal is not two miles ahead of us, in that direction," Bith said, pointing northeast. "He's closing rapidly with a large party of men; there are at least ten, perhaps twelve or more. I spotted them only the instant before that creature—"

"Then within moments those men will know of our presence," Endril interrupted. He pointed in the direction the wyvern had flown. Already it was descending out of sight behind a hill in the precise direction Bith had indicated. "That creature was a wyvern. If it comes again, beware the tail, for it contains a deadly poison."

"I do not think the flying thing will return," Hathor said bluntly. "If it does, I will kill it."

"There will be more than that beast to kill today," Endril predicted. "And Cal rides to certain death without our aid."

The elf said not one word more, but started at a gallop toward the peril that awaited them all.

"Yvaine. Yvaine. Yvaine . . ."

The word thudded over and over again through Cal's mind as his horse's hooves thudded over the damp road.

The foes were in sight now. There were ten, perhaps more. They had stopped just beyond a group of low mounds. As he closed the distance between them, the men moved quickly to form an impromptu battle line across the highway. The youth was no more than four hundred yards away when a huge beast screamed past him overhead, diving out of sight in the midst of the mounds.

No matter to Cal. Now his battle lust was fully aroused, and his only thoughts were of slaughter—and Yvaine. As he drew his sword and positioned his shield to guard his chest, he strained to see her, but could not.

Three hundred yards. Cal's heels dug into the horse's flanks, bringing the steed to a full gallop. The line of men before him parted, and a single man stepped forward to stand directly in the center of the road. Cal saw his full-length, plain white tunic, his large black cloak, and his upraised wooden staff.

Two hundred yards. Cal knew he was within archery range. None of the men pulled a bow. Why? The man in the black cloak began gesturing in a bizarre manner with his staff, waving it at the mounds to his right and left, and then pointing it at the roadway directly in front of the place where he stood.

One hundred yards. Cal screamed his battle cry, raised his sword, and braced for his first contact. . . .

His horse swerved, shrieked madly, reared, and fell. As the horse tumbled over to its left, Cal strained every muscle to throw his own body to the right. He crashed to the ground an instant after his horse but avoided landing beneath the beast.

Even as he was falling, Cal saw the hideous, mud-caked skeletal arms that had erupted from the earth to tangle themselves among his horse's legs. When he hit the ground, pain shot through his right arm and leg, but the pain he ignored, for a filthy hand erupted upward out of the mud not two inches from his eyes, and rotting, long-nailed fingers scratched at his metal helm. Behind him, Cal heard laughter, mocking laughter, from the man in the white tunic and black cloak.

"Behold," the man cried to his eager followers, "the mighty warrior come to attack us. And behold the power of your gods!"

A cheer erupted from the ranks of Cal's foes as the youth staggered to his feet. Cal sucked at the air, for the wind had been knocked from his lungs by his fall. Still, he managed to raise his sword and strike downward, cleaving the rotten arm that now grappled his leg.

More enemies were emerging from the very earth, clawing their way to the surface of the mounds all around him. Cal had no time to count his foes. He saw only their skeletal forms, some with rotten sinews, muscles, and flesh still attached in places. Many were armed: they carried large clubs, crude spears, stone axes. While Cal's senses cleared, these long-dead warriors gathered in front of the holy man who had summoned them.

"It is as well," Cal shouted, gasping for air between each word, "that the dead fight for you, for you shall soon join them!" He raised his sword high with both hands. "For

Rafael and Yvaine!" he screamed, charging into the thick of the walking dead.

Cal's blade flashed left and right, up and down. He struck with the flat of the blade, shattering ribs, and the edge, cleaving three and four skeletal forms in half with a single blow. In return, he received countless hits, as clubs and axes drove his chain mail into his rib cage, battered his greaves, and pounded his stomach. Blow after blow rained upon his steel-helmeted head. Cal staggered, stepped backward, then lurched forward again. He became insensate, incapable of feeling pain or fear. All that existed for Cal were his foes, his sword, and the need to wield the blade again and again and again.

He didn't stop swinging until he had sliced through nothing but air twice.

Then Cal paused, puzzled, because there were no more targets to strike. Battered heaps of twitching bones and broken skulls lay all about and beneath him. Blood, mingled with stinging sweat, poured over his eyes; rusty stains showed through the tunic beneath his chain mail; his brain registered the first tingles of pain. The roadway before him was clear for a distance of about one hundred feet. His original, living foes had retreated and re-formed a battle line. Shouting taunts at the wounded warrior, they brandished clubs, swords, and axes. Their leader stood to their rear, and Cal noticed that he glanced nervously several times toward the mounds, where the flying creature had apparently landed.

"Your gods," Cal called out, "are dead. They seem not to fare so well against the living. Give me the woman Yvaine, or you will join them."

"Our gods," their leader replied, "only toy with you. Here, meet another of the beings we praise."

With a nod of his head, the priest Garik (for it was he) called forth from their hiding place behind the mounds three horrid creatures of the same type that had fought Cal and Rafael's men. The dirty, shaggy-haired wights crept slowly into view, their great arms dragging against the ground,

their eyes squinted almost shut against the hated sunlight.
A cheer arose from the men in Garik's party, followed by
more taunting laughter.

The wights began to shamble forward, growling and
grunting, their sharp, fanglike teeth grinding as they antici-
pated human prey.

Great waves of pain wracked Cal's body, and his legs
began to tremble. Still, he stood his ground. Charging three
such creatures in his wounded condition would be suicidal.
He knew that no matter what he did, his chances of surviving
their attack were poor, but he judged it best to wait as they
approached and hope for some opening.

The three wights were less than ten paces away. Cal raised
his sword, ready to strike the leading creature, when a single
arrow whizzed past his head to bury itself in the monster's
chest. With a howl of agony the undead thing toppled over
backward.

"Greetings, Cal!" Endril's cheery voice came from atop
a mound just behind Cal.

"Endril!" Cal shouted.

"He is not alone," said Hathor, stepping into the road
behind Cal, "though I have lost my axe."

"It is the elf and the others. Charge them!" Garik
screamed.

With a shout, Garik's men surged forward. Endril let
fly one arrow, then another, and the remaining two wights
dropped before they could close with Cal. Hathor came
forward to fight, bare handed, at the youthful warrior's side,
while behind the two, Bith began tracing a large circle in
the roadway with the staff Hathor had cut for her.

In his wounded, exhausted state, Cal was hard pressed
when the charging men closed on him, but Hathor was
transformed into a frenzied, fighting beast. In his huge,
outstretched paws he grabbed two of the charging humans
by their hair, and with one powerful motion of his thick arms
crushed their skulls together. Cal struck down one man with
his sword, but received multiple blows that staggered him
and drove him backward.

"Cal, fall back!" Bith cried.

Cal quickly beat a fighting retreat backward several paces. His foes pressed thickly upon him until his feet stepped inside the circle Bith had made. Suddenly, he was free of his attackers. Three men beat vainly at the air before them, but their blows could not cross the invisible barrier formed by the enchantress's magic.

Endril's bowstring sang a song of death, and Hathor made short work of two of the remaining attackers. It was only as the last man dropped dead to the earth that Bith noticed the large wounded wyvern mounting rapidly into the sky, with the strangely clad man who had led their enemies riding its back.

"Look, Endril! Their leader escapes," Bith shouted.

Endril sent yet another arrow to seek the heart of the wyvern, but the angle for the shot was poor, and for the first time, Endril missed his mark. His second shot fell short, and as the frustrated elf watched in angry silence, the wyvern and its rider gradually disappeared from sight over the horizon to the north.

"Good friends, well met!" Cal said. Then he collapsed in a heap at Bith's feet.

"I hope his wounds are not serious," Endril said, approaching to examine the fallen fighter. "For there will be much more fighting, and bloodier, before this business is done."

"Then Cal will be glad to see this," Hathor interjected.

From the grasp of one of the dead men on the road, the troll removed the gleaming runesword Cal had won from Gunther Stedfyrd. He held the shining blade high in the midmorning sun for Bith and Endril to see.

"Vili is with us," the troll said, smiling.

CHAPTER
11

Love?

Cal awoke to find himself lying between warm blankets near a crackling campfire. Overhead, the full moon shed her pale, ruddy light down upon the foggy moor. Nearby, Bith, Endril, and Hathor talked quietly.

Cal groaned as he gained full consciousness.

"Ah, Caltus," Endril said, approaching with his customary, teasing grin. "Your chain mail served you well. You'll be sore for a long time, and I fear your ribs are cracked, but you will live to fight again another day."

"Thank you, Endril," Cal muttered. "Thank you all. If you had not been there . . ."

"If we had not been there, you would be dead and unable to give us the explanation you owe us," Bith stated flatly.

"Bith is right," Hathor said simply. "We waited for you, and then we searched for you. I am glad we found you, but I think it would be a good thing if you told us why you disappeared."

Cal groaned. His friends were right. He had ignored his duty to them. They had repaid him by being more than dutiful, rendering him good for evil; their loyalty, which he did not deserve, had saved his life.

The youth winced with pain as he struggled to sit up. His battered ribs made even the smallest movement agonizing. But more painful was the confession he now must make. He looked quietly for a moment at the faces of his three bold friends. There was no point in trying to avoid the full, simple truth.

"I fell in love," Cal said simply.

"You *what*?" Bith's voice had all the friendliness of a twanging bowstring.

"I feared as much," Endril said to no one in particular. The elf sighed and plopped down cross-legged on the ground.

"I couldn't help it," Cal said, speaking directly to Bith. "There was a fight, and I captured a runesword, and . . ."

"We know all that," Bith said impatiently. "You shouldn't have taken the job in the first place. Anyway, then your party was attacked, and you were wounded, and so forth. Get to the love part."

"I apologize to you all. I am truly sorry for keeping you waiting for me, and for not contacting you. I can only ask for your . . ." Cal paused, nearly choking on the word he had to say. "For your forgiveness," he said, wincing again with pain.

"Granted," Endril said quietly.

"I cannot be angry with Cal," Hathor said. "I do not understand what he means by this thing called falling in love, but I will not carry enmity for Cal for what he has done."

"It's not that easy, Cal." Bith's tone was sharp, and her eyes flashed in the firelight. "You abandoned your only good friends without warning. You endangered your own life and, indirectly, all of ours, because we had to come looking for you. Now, I want to know about your falling in love."

"Her name is Yvaine," Cal began. "Yvaine! Where is she? She was not with those we slew this morning?"

"No," Bith replied coolly. "We have not yet had the privilege of meeting this . . . merchant's daughter."

Bith practically spat the last two words at Cal. Endril flinched and ducked his head to hide his grin. Hathor looked to Endril, hoping for enlightenment, but found none in the elf's suppressed smile.

"But we must find her!" Cal tried to struggle to his feet, cried out loudly, and gently lowered himself back to the ground. "We must find her. She is wonderful, a wonderful, innocent, pure, beautiful, intelligent woman in the hands of those fiends! Where have they hidden her? Did you question them?"

"Calm yourself, Cal," Endril replied. "There is nothing to be done to help her tonight. We do not know her fate. In the heat of battle, we took no prisoners. Their leader escaped, but the girl was not with him."

"Oohh," Cal cried, close to tears, not from physical pain, but from frustrated rage and worry.

"Wonderful, innocent, pure, beautiful, and intelligent," Bith repeated. "Are you sure you're not omitting some important quality?"

"Bith, when we find her, you will see. She can do anything: she can read and write, and knows how to calculate. She can ride and fence. She has wisdom beyond her years."

"And obviously a certain amount of charm," Bith interjected.

"Oh, yes," Cal went on, not even noticing the sarcasm. "A great deal of charm. Her voice is like . . ."

Endril saw that Cal was likely to continue in the same vein until sleep overpowered him. Silently, the elf stood and started to slip away from the fire. Hathor rose and followed him. The two walked in silence over the empty moor. Cal's voice droned on and on behind them.

"I think," Endril said when the two were finally beyond earshot of Bith and Cal, "that Bith will learn more about the celebrated Yvaine than she wanted to know."

"I do not understand," Hathor said, a question in his voice.

"It is love, Hathor. Human love."

Hathor's mouth screwed up and his eyes moved closer together. Wrinkles appeared on his brow beneath his tousled red hair. He stood silent for several moments. "What is human love?" the troll asked at last.

Endril looked away, his eyebrows raised to the heavens. *This could be difficult,* the elf thought. "Well," he began, "don't trolls choose mates?"

"Trolls mate," Hathor said, nodding his huge head.

"Well, there you are," Endril said with a wink, hoping this explanation would suffice.

"Where am I?" Hathor asked.

Ah, well, Endril thought. A simple explanation had been worth a try. "Love is what humans feel when they desire to mate," he said, taking a second stab at explaining what he himself hardly understood.

Hathor pondered this for a time. "Cal desires offspring?" he finally asked.

"I doubt that," Endril said.

"Then why does he desire to mate?" Hathor asked, eagerness for knowledge beaming from his face. "And why does that explain why he left us?"

"For humans, mating is only a part of love. What Cal really wants is to be with this one woman, Yvaine."

"Then he no longer wants to be in our company?" Hathor frowned, sadly.

"No, no. Of course Cal still wants to be with us," Endril said. He knew this would be an important point for Hathor.

"Ah, then, Cal wants us all to be with Yvaine."

"No, not exactly. Cal wants Yvaine to be his mate, his only mate, for life. He also wants her to be his closest companion. But he does not wish to abandon us. We're his good friends."

Hathor nodded appreciatively. Then his eyes lit up again as a new thought occurred to him. "But Cal did abandon us," Hathor pointed out.

"Yes, yes," Endril said, his patience growing short. "But he didn't want to. I mean, he did want to, but he didn't want to at the same time. He was not thinking well. Humans in love often do not think well."

"I see," Hathor said, a broad, toothy smile of understanding crossing his face. "Love is a sickness of the mind."

"Just so," Endril said cheerily. "You've got it."

"Yes," Hathor replied, beaming happily. "Love is like wanting to eat meat."

CHAPTER
12

Night Visions

Hathor and Endril walked slowly back toward the fire. Bith's and Cal's voices still drifted on the night air. Long before they were close enough to understand the words being spoken, the elf and the troll could tell that Bith was working up a fine fit of temper. This was a battle that all of Cal's prowess with arms would not help him win.

"But, Bith," Cal was pleading, "what can I do? I am ashamed of the way I treated you, Endril, and Hathor. I crave your friendship. At the same time, I must continue to seek Yvaine. Please, help me."

"Have you lost all reason?" Bith shouted. "Your pursuit of this golden-haired heiress has almost cost us all our lives. Endril says there is some great evil afoot that requires our immediate action. What of your duty to us? Oh, I had forgotten. There is no *beauty* to keep you attached to us."

"Bith," Hathor said, stepping into the firelight, "do not be harsh with Cal." The troll leaned close to Bith and tried, as best a troll could, to whisper in her ear. "He has a sickness."

"It seems to me that his wounds are well deserved," Bith sullenly responded, missing Hathor's meaning.

121

"He is also wounded," Hathor began, preparing to patiently explain his new understanding of love.

"And both his sickness and his wounds might heal more readily if he saw our trophy from today's battle," Endril offered.

"The sword! I had forgotten," Hathor said. The troll rummaged through a great sack that contained many edible roots and miscellaneous other gear. "Here, Cal. See what we recovered from the men who attacked you."

Firelight glittered off the great rune-inscribed blade as the troll lifted it high for Cal to see.

"My runesword! With such a weapon, I cannot fail to rescue Yvaine!" Cal's face lit up with joy as he took the weapon from Hathor's hand. "The men we fought today must have been the same who attacked Rafael on the way to Dralton. That man in the white tunic—he must be the holy man Yvaine said was their leader."

"He is a priest of sorts," Endril said. "But there is nothing holy about him. He serves an ancient, filthy cult that makes gods of monsters, and monsters of men."

"Was it this cult that the travelers at our inn described to you?" Bith asked, suddenly suspecting that the cult was the evil Endril had predicted they must face.

"Yes," the elf replied. "It is spreading again. Already the kingdom of Trondholm in the far north is falling under its sway. Its followers worship the undead as gods. They practice vile rites, and they spread ruin to all lands that adopt their ways."

"Then you think this cult is part of some plan of the Dark Lord's," Bith said, her anger at Cal forgotten for the moment.

"That is almost certain. From what the travelers told me, I would guess that by midsummer Trondholm will be attacked, and the Mistwall will roll forward to claim that fair realm for the Dark Lord's domain."

"Then we go north," Hathor said.

"It is not that simple, Hathor. We must oppose this evil, and we will try to help Trondholm if we can," Endril said.

"But you saw today the power of this cult. That simple priest called forth the dead from their burial mounds to fight for him. And wights—we were fortunate the ones he summoned were small and weak. Few wights can be dispatched with a single silvered arrow. I trust you have not forgotten the powers of the other undead that I spoke of last night. To go north would be to go directly to the great source of this cult's power. What could we four hope to accomplish against them? No. We must have a more subtle approach."

"What do you suggest?" Bith asked.

"I do not know," Endril replied. "I had hoped that Vili would help us, show us a way. . . ."

A voice boomed in the midst of the camp. "At last you call upon me, arrogant elf," it said.

"The sword!" Cal exclaimed, lifting it high above him, his face contorted from the pain of his effort. The face of the god took shape amid the runes on the blade, and the voice continued to speak, its deep tones echoing hauntingly.

"I see that you are ready to acknowledge your need for me," the voice said.

"Exalted Ruler," Bith quickly responded, "I thank you for your aid this day." Bith's opinion of Vili had improved substantially since the spell he had taught her the night before had worked so well today.

"Ah, a human who knows how to speak with a god."

"Yes, Exalted One, the human thanks you for your magic, and I thank you as well. Long have I thought you would call upon us," Endril said.

"You called upon me!"

"As you say," Endril agreed. "What task would you place before us?"

"Find the girl, Yvaine, daughter of Rafael, and Trondholm will be saved," the voice replied. "Seek her in the far north, where the Mistwall touches the Bloody Range."

"Exalted High Ruler," Endril said, doubt creeping into his voice, "what connection could there be between this simple girl and the Dark Lord's threat to Trondholm?

Surely she is but an innocent victim of a great evil that—"

"Enough!" the voice shouted. Vili's face in the sword contorted in rage. "I have given you your task, and my promise! Is the promise of a god not enough for you?"

"There was a previous matter of reward," Hathor volunteered.

"You insubordinate creatures try my patience. You have my command, my constant aid, and my promise. It is enough."

The sword glowed brilliantly bright for an instant, and the image disappeared from view. Cal let the blade drop by his side. The four companions were silent for a long while.

"Find the girl?" Bith finally muttered. "Has she charmed gods as well as . . . boys?"

"Surely, Bith, even you must agree that we should obey the command of a god," Cal said, smiling despite his pain. "With the help of Vili, I'll be able to travel by morning."

"The god is with us," Hathor said. "And if we must fight undead monsters, we are fortunate to have Endril with us. Endril knows all about these things."

"That is true," Bith agreed. "At least we will have knowledge of our foes. Tell us, Endril, how is it that you learned so much about these creatures?"

Endril did not answer.

CHAPTER
13

Secrets

As spring's promise of new life found fulfillment in early summer, the four companions journeyed northward. In times past, their journeys together had been filled with both adventure and laughter; this trip was different.

Cal's wounds slowly healed, with the help of time and a touch of both medicine and magic from the hands of Bith and Endril. But Cal's thoughts and speech were always and ever the same: the rescue of Yvaine was his only theme. Elizebith avoided Cal more and more; she rode far behind him, and her conversation with him was limited to the few exchanges of mundane information necessitated by their travels. Endril showed little of his typical mischievous mirth. The elf, often as not, rode silently, brooding over some matter his three friends could only imagine. Only Hathor seemed his usual self. By day he kept the rear guard; by night he chewed his roots and worked on making a new axe for himself from a sturdy wooden haft and a great stone. Every night he shaped the stone, chipping the edges finer and finer, until the weapon was sharper than many a neglected blade of steel. But gradually, as he thought through all the things Endril had said, the troll came to believe that he and his friends were traveling toward certain death.

From time to time, always in the cool of the early night, the face of Vili would appear in the blade of Cal's runesword, and the voice of the god would urge the foursome to hasten their pace toward Trondholm and the Bloody Range. Finding Yvaine as quickly as possible seemed to be of paramount importance to the god. Little enthusiasm greeted Vili's appearances. Each time Vili spoke, Endril's pensive, taciturn mood grew darker, Bith's temper grew shorter, and Hathor's doubts grew greater. Only Cal responded eagerly to each appearance of the god; the youth even learned to show respect and obeisance in the divine presence.

"It's fine for Cal to become so devoted to Vili now," Bith confided to Hathor. "It's pretty easy to be devoted to someone who orders your friends to do what you want them to."

"A god's ways are not our ways," Hathor commented, feeling curiously wise, "but our ways must become the ways commanded by the gods. As for Cal, you must remember he is sick. Perhaps it is fortunate that Vili wants the same thing Cal wants. What would happen if Cal, in his sickness, were to oppose Vili?"

Bith shook her head sadly and resumed her sullen silence.

The four pressed on, passing through the populated farming regions of the central plains. Usually they avoided the villages, both to minimize word of their own passage north, in case any foe should have an interest, and to avoid trouble for Hathor. Still, Cal, Bith, or Endril would leave the party briefly once every few days to visit a village market or a country inn, purchasing with their meager remaining funds a few supplies and keeping a keen eye and ear out for information.

Cal returned to his friends' camp near daybreak one morning, having spent the previous evening and night on such a mission.

"The numbers of people traveling down from Trondholm grows greater daily," he reported. "And in the village, I saw a curious custom. The residents here put a small plate outside their door or window before going to sleep. On each of these plates is a handful of gold or copper coins or a bit of bloody meat or some other small thing of value. In the morning, these items are gone, yet none are accused of their theft. This custom is new to me."

"It is no custom, but part of the worship of the cult whose destruction we seek," Endril said. "The items set out at night are offerings to the undead, to keep the dwellers in the house safe for the night."

"Ah, then, that explains the presence of several men clad in that strange costume—the one worn by the leader of those we fought. The white tunic, black cloak, and—"

"You saw men such as these?" Bith asked. "Why didn't you take one prisoner and bring him here? Perhaps he could tell us more about the fate of your precious Yvaine or provide information we need about our enemies. Really, Cal, what is the matter with you? You would never have hesitated before."

"Of course I considered doing that very thing," Cal said, unperturbed. His hand came to rest on the hilt of the runesword that he now wore constantly. "But I sensed that to do so would be against the will of Vili."

"Why so?" Endril asked in as offhand a manner as he could manage.

"Because . . ." Cal paused. Bith's suggestion made sense. Why had he decided not to take these men prisoner, find out what he could from them about Yvaine, and then slay the lot of them? That was the natural thing, the proper thing, the smart thing to do. Yet Cal could find in himself not even the smallest amount of anger toward these so-called holy men. He had no desire to harm them or even interfere with them. Perhaps they were not the real enemy, he thought. Vili simply wanted Yvaine found, just as Cal did. Perhaps this cult was a sidetrack of some sort.

"Because," Cal finally continued, "it just would be against the will of the god. Vili's interest is Yvaine. The cult is secondary." Cal saw the look of consternation that flashed for a moment on Endril's face. "Anyway," he added quickly, relieved to have suddenly thought of something more to say, "why alert them to our presence by attacking or kidnapping or killing their priests?"

Bith, Hathor, and Endril all exchanged serious glances. Cal's behavior was so strange, so contrary to both his nature and common sense, that all three feared he was becoming seriously deranged.

Cal saw the looks they exchanged and tried to retrieve the situation by a show of enthusiastic bravado. "Well, good friends, let's ride! Our goal is still many days' travel, and the sun is already up. Come on! When the time is right, the god will tell us to strike, and we will rescue Yvaine and save a kingdom!"

Cal guided his steed steadily forward toward the line of high hills on the horizon. The moors were now miles behind, and the party had entered the foothills of the northern mountains. The road, once straight, began to twist and turn, passing for a while through farmlands, then curving up and down wooded slopes of increasingly steeper grade. So far the woods were light, with fine hardwood trees and little underbrush. Atop the taller hills ahead, cedars and pines reared, and the forest floor grew thicker.

They just don't understand, Cal thought of his companions. He had to admit to himself that sometimes *he* didn't understand, either. He tried again to think through the short conversation of this morning. Now, Bith's question was a reasonable, sensible . . .

No, he told himself. Nothing mattered but Yvaine. Prisoners and skirmishes would be sideshows, distractions that would keep them from the main goal. Besides, if priests of this cult that Endril seemed so concerned about suddenly started disappearing, the enemy would know that something was afoot. It would just make the rescue of Yvaine that much more difficult.

Cal urged a little more speed from his mount. His three companions were strung out along the road behind him, as always. Why didn't they have more enthusiasm for this quest? Couldn't they understand a simple thing like love? Didn't he have the god Vili's own command to rescue the girl? Hadn't the runesword been returned to them? No foe, not even a vampire, could stand against that powerful weapon. Especially when that weapon was used by someone with Cal's prowess! Weren't these companions still his friends?

Of course, Cal suddenly thought, they may not completely trust me. My earlier behavior was wrong. Maybe they fear I'll abandon them again, or make some costly error in battle. Shame reddened Cal's face as he remembered the day of his rescue by the threesome. To need their aid in battle was not shameful, but to have to apologize and try to explain his inmost feelings . . .

And Bith! What was wrong with that woman? She was so full of anger. Everything Cal suggested displeased her. She had never even said she accepted his apology. Something would have to be done about Bith, Cal thought. Her constant, sullen dissension could endanger their mission. It could endanger Yvaine's life.

As the taller hills ahead came into closer view, Cal sighed. Yvaine would have loved this view. The hills were steeper than those of her homeland, but they had a wild beauty she would have much enjoyed. She would have delighted at the thick growths of hardwood trees that mottled their sides and the patches of woodland flowers certain to be found in the sunny patches of those forests. How her face would have shined in the early-morning light as the sun peeped over those hilltops! Indeed, Cal thought, the sun would consider itself fortunate to have her face to shine upon.

They would reach the high hill before nightfall, Cal judged. Then a few more days, and they would ascend into the mountains proper, crossing the border into Trondholm. Endril had said that the Bloody Range was a great mountain just to the north of that kingdom, a kind of rocky sentinel between the kingdom and the Mistwall just beyond.

Well, soon all would be well. Vili would lead them to the rescue of Yvaine. Hathor's spirits would improve with success in battle. Endril would certainly stop his brooding once Trondholm was saved, as Vili promised. As for Bith . . . Something would have to be done about Bith. A peculiar, unknown, evil sensation shot through Cal. For a brief instant a very dark thought strayed through his mind, the thought of how the runesword would feel as it sliced through Bith! He dismissed the thought in a moment as nonsense. Still, he felt strangely thrilled.

"Endril, I have a question."

Hathor had left his post at the rear of their little column and ridden forward to join the elf for a bit of private conversation. Perhaps, he thought, Endril would be more communicative or at least in a better mood. After all, there were trees around now.

"What is your question, good troll? Are you wondering if the people of Trondholm build large bakeries in their villages?" Endril's attempt at humor fell flat. It was useless to feign mirth when one felt none, the elf decided.

"No, that is not my question," Hathor replied matter-of-factly. "My question, is one I hesitate to ask."

"I will take no offense," the elf reassured him, "though I may choose not to answer," he added, his tone growing more grave.

"Why do you conceal from us much of what you know?" Hathor asked calmly.

"What do you mean?" Endril replied, dodging the troll's question.

"You know about Cal's sickness," Hathor began. "You know the types of foes we will meet, their powers and their weaknesses. You know the path to the Bloody Range, where not even trolls are accustomed to tread. You know about this cult that does such evil things. And you know we will surely die in our attempt to fight them, unless Vili helps us more than he ever has before."

"All true," Endril agreed cautiously.

"To know all these things, you must know some other thing. There is something that ties all these things together. What is it? And how do you know it?"

The troll's abilities in logic are definitely improving, the elf thought quietly.

"There are some things one does not speak of unless a higher good demands it," Endril said flatly.

Hathor nodded slowly, then dropped back to take up his position as rear guard once again.

CHAPTER
14

Raising Troops

Malendor unrolled a sheet of thick parchment across the top of the richly grained wooden table. His black eyes gazed upon the map of Trondholm, and he eagerly scanned the arrows and markings that showed the paths of planned troop movements, the locations for local revolts, and scheduled uprisings of orc tribes. Beneath the map itself, in the strangely twisted characters of an alphabet known only to the Dark Lord's most trusted servants, a list of the forces to be used and a schedule for their movement spelled the final doom of Trondholm.

The dark elf smiled maliciously. The plan was solid. Already Trondholm was rotted from within. Only a handful would remain loyal to the old ways, and only a few of that handful would have the courage left to fight. This plan would cause them to gather in one place, where they could be conveniently killed.

On the appointed day, the Mistwall would open and the Dark Lord's human troops would be unleashed. Raiding parties would scatter through the valleys, working their way from the northeastern and northwestern corners of the kingdom toward a central point. Meanwhile, the bulk of the army would concentrate at the foot of the Ochre Mountain. Then, one mighty thrust through the mountain passes would place them squarely in the center of the kingdom. Any who hoped to oppose them would have to meet them there, or the bulk of the kingdom would be conquered by default.

When the enemy concentrated for battle, Malendor's own special forces would come into play. On the moonless eve of the destruction of whatever army Trondholm could muster, the dark elf's undead minions would attack the enemy encampment. Insubstantial shadows would flit unseen through the night, infiltrating the enemy, spreading cold death with their mere touch. Zombies would make the main assault, their clumsiness compensated for by magic, which would hasten their movements. Overhead, wights mounted on wyverns would descend to spread further confusion and death in the foe's ranks. Overall command would be in Malendor's own hands. A coven of vampires and trusted priests of his own cult would serve as his staff. Before the morning's light, the army of Trondholm would be but a memory. Then the Dark Lord's human forces could roll forward unopposed, mopping up any local resistance.

Even that would be minimal, Malendor judged. Orc risings in the mountains would occupy the handful of dwarves and elves who could never accept the Dark Lord's victory. And in most villages, Malendor's loyal Friends of Eternal Life would welcome the incoming troops as liberators and friends. Victory would be total, complete, and irrevocable.

Then Malendor would spring his great surprise on the Dark Lord himself. Why stop? The Friends of Eternal Life could be called upon to rise in the hill country to the south, all the way down to the vast central plains. With the mountain barrier of Trondholm breached, and their way paved by friendly revolts, the Dark Lord's forces could march inexorably south, sweeping all before them as far as the moor country.

Malendor sat down and studied the map carefully one more time. It was perfect. His pale white hand tapped the parchment with satisfaction.

"Yes," the dark elf muttered.

But there was one victory that would be even sweeter.

He looked up from the map and swept his eyes around the clutter of his secret study and laboratory. In the light of the single sputtering torch on the far wall he surveyed the piles of tomes of ancient and evil magic. He saw the dusty shelves with their little vials of potions, herbs, roots, animal parts, and other things, vile and stinking, used in the practice of his black art. He admired his worktables laden with beakers, forceps, scales, and measures of all kinds. His gaze came to rest upon the great chest in the far corner, wherein he stored his great treasure trove of magical items and his personal ceremonial robes.

Endril would see this room before he died, Malendor decided. The plan was working perfectly.

A soft tapping at the single door to this secret chamber, located behind the great throne, intruded on Malendor's musings.

That would be Yvaine. She alone, besides himself and one other, knew of this room. He had shown her every possible kindness and courtesy; he had wooed her mind and soul, and now, he reflected, she was so completely his, she was a kind of bride.

"Enter," he called.

The door swung open silently. Yvaine glided in, her steps making no sound on the stone floor. Her face and belly were bloated, and trickles of rich blood dribbled down her chin. She had just fed.

"Is it time?" she asked, her once-delicate voice now a raspy hiss.

"Yes, my beloved little immortal," Malendor replied, careful to keep the tone of mockery out of his voice. He extended his arm toward her, and their two cold hands touched lightly at the fingertips. "It is time to raise our forces for the invasion of Trondholm. You may stand by my side."

A deadly smile of pure evil glee crossed Yvaine's bloody face. Malendor rose and went to the great chest. He muttered a single word, and the lid silently opened. The dark elf removed a long, full cloak made of rich, thick velvet, trimmed with gold. This he put on over his pure white tunic, clasping it with a great gold clasp encrusted with small diamonds around a large, blood red ruby. Lastly, he removed from the chest a gold chain. Hanging on that chain was a single, large, finely cut gemstone, black as jet, yet opaque. The stone glittered and glistened in an undefinable way, as though a black flame burned within it. Of his many enchanted items, this was his favorite, and greatest. He wore it often.

Malendor placed the chain around his neck so that the stone hung perfectly in the center of his chest. His long, white fingers gently stroked the black amulet, and a shudder of pure pleasure ran through his body. The thrill of victory would be great, he thought, and the thrill of his revenge on Endril even greater. But not even those sensations could compare with what he felt at this moment: sheer, raw, absolute destructive power over the bodies and souls of the living and the dead.

"My lord," the beautiful blond vampire behind him croaked in her broken, evil voice. "I love you."

Malendor's laughter exploded so loudly that it could be heard echoing in the great, cavernous throne room.

"No doubt you do, my sweet; no doubt you do," Malendor whispered back. Then his laughter exploded again, and the Lord on Earth of the Undead abandoned himself for a few brief moments to the enjoyment of a total, joyful, purely evil rapture.

Garik was beside himself with excitement. He stood just to the left of the Exalted One, Malendor himself, directly in front of the great throne. Magical orbs floated high above the floor of the huge cavern room below, bathing the scene with an eerie sort of illumination that could not truly be called light. Two rows of white-robed, black-cloaked holy men of the Friends of Eternal Life lined the three hundred steps to the great throne, their faces rapt with attention to

Malendor's every word. At the foot of the stairs, the stone altar stood cold and bare, but Garik knew that before the hour was out it would be drenched with steaming blood. Malendor's moment of triumph approached. He would call forth great gods today, great gods who would serve both him and the Friends in the conquest of Garik's homeland.

So great was Garik's anticipation that he did not even mind sharing his position of honor with the blond vampiress who stood to Malendor's right. Why the Exalted One so favored her Garik did not fully understand, though he knew that in some way, she played a crucial role in Malendor's plan. Well, Garik, too, had played a role in that plan, a key role. Today he would receive his just reward.

"And now the gods will walk among you," Malendor cried to his followers. "Look well upon the stone floor below."

Garik's eyes joined those of the six hundred other assembled holy men. He strained to see what Malendor indicated, but the large cavern room itself was empty; the stone floor was bare.

Then Malendor spoke a word of command in a strange tongue, and the solid stone floor in the center of the room vanished. Where once there had been solid rock—rock that every man present had walked upon—a vast, deep pit now gaped. From the pit arose a stench of death so powerful that dozens of the holy men fainted outright. The rest clutched their stomachs and placed hands over their suddenly pale faces. In the pit were countless corpses, the mangled remains of men, elves, dwarves, orcs, gnomes, and other beings Garik could not identify. They were piled one atop another in a gruesome display. Rotted limbs tangled together; skeletal arms wrapped around one another as if in mortal combat. Some of the dead had been freshly killed; bloated, rotting flesh still clung to their bones. Others had been dead . . . how long? It was impossible to tell.

"Behold the material from which we, Friends, will create our own gods!" Malendor's voice rose in pitch and volume. Despite his revulsion, Garik felt a strange thrill of obscene excitement as he listened to the dark elf's words. "For centuries some of these dead have lain in wait, silently, mindlessly, patiently, and . . ." Malendor could not suppress a smile as he uttered the next word. " . . . faithfully. They were awaiting the events of this day. Now your living eyes will behold what their dead ones have longed to see. Garik!"

The priest startled.

"Exalted One?" he replied.

"Stand before me," Malendor invited, stepping back to make room for the man on the very edge of the top step. "Turn and gaze into the very substance of the gods."

Garik did as he was commanded. Utterly fascinated, he stared down into the pit, while the recovering holy men along the steps gazed up at him. Behind Garik, Malendor raised a short, curved ceremonial blade.

"Garik has served me well," Malendor said in a low tone. "He has earned the reward of immortality. But he will not become a mere zombie or wight; he will not become even a powerful vampire. His reward shall be greater than that."

Garik gasped. His heart thudded. What joy, what special honor, what unparalleled power did the master intend to give him?

"Garik will live in all these gods, for from his blood, they shall be made!" Malendor exclaimed.

With a sudden swipe of the sharp steel blade, the dark elf neatly severed Garik's head. The priest's face still held its expression of horrified surprise as Malendor pitched the head down into the pit. Then he lifted the body high and hurled it downward, too, using a precast spell to control its flight so that it crashed in a mangled heap directly upon the altar stone. Garik's blood gushed in great, steaming gouts from the severed arteries to drip down the sides of the altar and trickle into the pit.

"And now," Malendor cried, gripping the black stone on the chain around his neck and lifting it before his face, "let our gods and our armies arise!"

Not even Malendor's trained priests could suppress their screams of horror as the corpses in the pit became a writhing mass and the stinking dead began to claw their way up the sides of their granite mass grave.

CHAPTER
15

Invasion

"Soon, the great struggle will begin."

The speaker sat in a slightly raised, large, plain chair that marked the head of the round council table. He shrugged slightly, seeming smaller than he truly was in the bulky, thick purple robe and cloak that were the necessary ceremonial attire of the elected king of Trondholm. The man looked away from the table, and across the large, airy room to the view of Trondholm's high mountains, which appeared in the wood-framed square windows. He loved this kingdom. Now he would have to decide how best to defend it.

"It has begun already!" A burly knight's mailed fist hammered down on the map of the kingdom spread out on the table. "The Mistwall parts on our northeastern and northwestern borders. Their raiders are pouring through our passes even as we speak."

"Then what do you counsel your king?" Alfred the Red-Haired demanded. "How many knights have we? How many villagers have responded to the summoning of the fyrd?"

The king's angry eyes moved from face to face around the table.

"It is one thing to demand action," Alfred said. "It is another to decide what action to take."

The knight whose speech had roused the king's irritation held his ground.

"The foe is here and here," he said, indicating two widely separated points upon the map of Trondholm. "Honor demands that some force oppose them. We cannot change the fact that our resources are meager. But we can fight and die like men of courage. I counsel you to send what forces we have at once to challenge the invaders on both fronts."

"To divide our small numbers would be folly," countered a bearded warrior. "First we should strike one of the enemy columns with all our strength, then countermarch to defeat the second force."

The assembled leading warriors of Trondholm grunted and nodded in agreement. Alfred the Red-Haired shook his head in amazement.

"Friends," he reasoned, "pride has robbed you of all sense. Perhaps you can afford to let wounded honor dictate your course of action, but I cannot, for this nation lives or dies by my decision. Think well on the plain facts. Of experienced knights, professional leaders of fighting of men, we have only a handful. Most are sitting at this table now, and I count fifteen of you here."

The king paused to let this fact sink into the skulls of these well-meaning, well-armed, but not overly brilliant men.

"Our command to raise the fyrd," the king continued, "has produced less than one-fourth the troops we would have hoped to command. Many of our people are frankly disloyal, and many more of our best men have fled south to find havens for their families. We have no time to raise mercenary soldiers."

Alfred's audience sat in sullen silence. They knew the king spoke sense, but their natural reaction to a crisis was fighting, not thinking.

"Further consider," the king said, "that these invaders are, so far, raiding parties. The enemy has not yet revealed the location or the direction of march of his main force. If we divide what few troops we have, or exhaust them in countermarches through our mountains, what chance will we have when the main attack is made?"

"We have no chance no matter what our strategy," a young knight offered flatly. "Our only choices are to fight and die, or to surrender and die. I would prefer to fight."

"Well said," spoke another knight, and murmurs of agreement rose around the table.

"Then it is not I, whom you accuse of inaction, who surrenders this kingdom, but you!" Alfred said, his rage rising again.

"My lord."

The guard at the door of the counsel room entered boldly.

"What now?" the king shouted, diverting his anger onto the hapless man.

"There are strangers here, brought all the way from our southern border where the central highway crosses it. They claim to have knowledge that would be invaluable against the invaders. They have been interrogated thoroughly. The captain of your personal guard begs you to hear them at once."

The king hestiated only a moment. This strategy meeting was producing no desirable results. Perhaps a recess would allow tempers to cool, including his own. And new information could be valuable. . . .

"My lords," the king said to the assembled knights, "we will resume our discussions after the midday meal."

"Why are we wasting our time here?" Cal shouted angrily at Endril. The youth paced back and forth in the empty hallway. He felt like sticking his dagger into one of the large wooden beams that supported the white walls. The two royal guards nearby watched him carefully but did not move. "We are not going to defeat the cult of the . . . whatever they call themselves. . . ."

"The Friends of Eternal Life is their current name," Endril said dryly. The elf did not wish to provoke a nasty scene here, in the royal residence of Trondholm. It had taken all his powers to gain his companions this audience with the king. If only Cal would calm himself and be silent!

"Well, we aren't going to defeat them by force of arms," Cal insisted. "Vili says we must find Yvaine to save this kingdom. But for four days we have put up with being escorted here, to meet their silly king, at your insistence. We've been searched, questioned, and insulted. And we've done nothing, nothing at all to find Yvaine!"

Cal was dangerously angry at the elf now, Hathor judged. If this rift was not soon healed, the human would attack Endril. Hathor knew too that Bith was very near the point where she might act with poor judgment. He feared she might attack Cal with some form of magic before Cal attacked Endril. All in all, the troll thought, things were not going well. They had not gone well ever since the group crossed the border into this kingdom. From that moment, Endril had done everything possible to gain the ear of its king. Hathor did not know, but he suspected that some of the elf's magic, especially the way he had of making people like and trust him, had played a large part in their gaining this audience.

Endril held his temper in check.

"Cal, we must talk with this king to gain information on the movement of the Dark Lord's forces and the progress of the invasion. We are fortunate to be here, where we can learn all we need to know from the most reliable source. With the information we gain, we will stand a better chance of finding Yvaine," the elf said patiently.

Cal paced back and forth some more. Why couldn't Endril understand? They should be searching for Yvaine. Absolutely nothing else mattered. . . .

"The king will see you now."

"Oh, very well," Cal said glumly. "Let's get this over with."

"I will require your weapons," the guard said firmly. "No stranger may stand armed before the king."

All of Endril's persuasive powers, and several deadly stares from Bith, were required to convince Cal to hand over the runesword, which had not left his side since the night Hathor handed it back to him.

"Why should I trust strangers who appear mysteriously upon my borders just as my kingdom is invaded? Especially when one of those strangers is neither man nor elf, but obviously . . ."

"You have no reason to trust us. But our words may make sufficient sense that you will do as we suggest based on your own free decision," Endril replied simply.

"No reason to trust us!" Cal blurted out rudely. "Let's not forget that we happen to be the ones who blunted the Dark Lord's attack the last time the Mistwall parted. Let's not forget about defeating the Queen of Ice, and let's not forget about the battle of—"

"I have heard of you," Alfred Red-Haired said suddenly. "So it is true. A small group of adventurers have more than once defeated the Dark Lord. You are the heroes of Cairngorm."

"Of course it's true," Cal said curtly. "Now, Endril, let's get on with this. We have a mission of our own that requires our attention."

"Be patient, Cal. Lord King, what movements have the Dark Lord's armies made?" Endril asked.

"It is no secret," the king responded. "Here, look at the map for yourselves."

As Endril suspected, Cal could not help but come to glance at the map.

"Here, Cal, is the Bloody Range," Endril explained. "It lies beyond the border of Trondholm and separates that kingdom's north-central region from the Mistwall. But I know from a time long past that there are endless tunnels though that mountain. An entire army could travel through there unseen, to emerge at the head of this valley. . . ."

"And the raiding parties have struck here and here," Cal muttered, becoming intrigued by the strategic problem.

"Hmmm. The raids are a feint obviously, designed to draw off strength. See, if the Trondholmers move against the raiders, they well have fewer forces to oppose a main thrust here, through the pass from the Bloody Range directly into the center of the kingdom," Cal continued, warming to his topic. "This point here," he said, putting his finger on the very place where Malendor planned to fight his main battle, "is the key. If the enemy seizes it, they control the access to five of the seven major valleys. They cannot take this point."

"I see," Endril said cautiously. It was working. Cal was thinking about battle and the movement of troops. His advice would be invaluable. "So you think the Trondholm army should concentrate at this key point?"

"Of course not," Cal replied. "The enemy can read a map as well as we. To fight a defensive battle at that point is probably what they would expect Trondholm to do. They will be prepared to win that battle."

"Then what would you suggest?" the king inquired. Whoever this rude young man might be, he had a good mind for the movements of armies.

"Well, as your forces are greatly inferior in numbers, I would say you must win the fight before the enemy's main strength can be brought to bear. We're assuming the enemy plans a massive thrust south to the center of the kingdom and plans to destroy you in a defensive battle there. Don't play his game. Attack him somewhere near here," Cal suggested, growing more excited as he pointed out the place where the Dark Lord's forces could be expected to emerge from the Bloody Range. "Hit the enemy in his assembly areas with total surprise, and you will find that a small force, effectively led, can defeat a disorganized, partly assembled army ten times its own size."

"And what if our assumption about the enemy's intentions is wrong?" Alfred asked.

"Then your own army is still intact and untouched," Cal replied. "If the enemy advances from any point other than through the Bloody Range, you can be in his rear in two days of forced marches."

"Cal," Bith said, genuine surprise in her voice, "that's brilliant." She had forgotten in recent weeks how skilled Cal could be.

"One thing must be added," Endril said. "The foe will undoubtedly employ monstrous undead creatures among his forces. Avoid combat by night, and if there are any mages in this kingdom, let them use their power to give courage to your own troops. Many brave men will flee at the mere sight of these creatures, so fearsome is their presence."

"Of magic we have little," Alfred said, "just as we have little of everything that is needful, except weapons. Our men will have to confront these things with no courage but their own. Still, under our joint leadership, with careful timing so we do not fight in the darkness, this plan may work."

"Our joint leadership?" Cal asked.

"Yes," Alfred replied. "You trust your own plan, do you not?"

"Certainly," Cal snapped rudely. "But I have another task to accomplish."

"Cal," Endril said, "where did Vili say to find Yvaine?"

"In the Bloody Range, as you know full well."

"What better way to go there than at the head of an army?" the elf asked.

A smile of understanding spread slowly across Cal's face. Hathor glanced at Bith and saw her heave a sigh of relief that the tension between Cal and Endril was ending. *This is better,* thought the troll. *Now we have only several hordes of zombies and vampires to deal with.*

CHAPTER
16

The Second Battle
Of Bloody Range

King Alfred the Red-Haired was happy despite the danger facing his beloved Trondholm. He had a plan in which he had confidence. He had new allies in the heroes of Cairngorm (for word of that episode had finally spread even to his far northern land). He had a small force of united and happy knights—happy because their king was leading them into battle, which they felt honor required.

Cal was happy, too. He was riding toward a battle that could lead to the rescue of Yvaine. He rode next to a king, who paid respect to his views on military matters, and he rode at the head of an army. He wasn't its commander, and it wasn't really much of an army. In fact, the entire host of Trondholm consisted of twenty knights with about two hundred mounted retainers and some eight hundred men on foot who had answered the call-up of the fyrd. A handful of wizards, some hags and strange holy men who served the local gods, and the usual hangers-on completed the assemblage. *No matter, though,* thought Cal. *It's still an army, and I'm still riding at its head.*

Alfred had proved a generous leader. If the numbers of his forces were small, they were nevertheless well equipped. Cal

146

wore a fine new suit of plate armor, worthy of a knight, and on his new helm and great shield the traditional arms of the kings of Trondholm identified him as a high royal retainer. At his side Cal wore a long sword presented to him by the king, though he wore this reluctantly. He would much rather have the runesword on his person; still, courtesy required that he honor the king's gift—until fighting began.

There was even a boy assigned to Cal as a sort of squire. Of course, he wasn't really a squire, for Cal was not truly a knight. Still, the boy bore Cal's arms, including the precious runesword. He had charge of Cal's new mount, a true northern warhorse. Cal found that the boy would readily do whatever Cal ordered, provided the orders weren't complicated. If the youth, whose name was Orlac, was a bit dense, he made up for this shortcoming with a single-minded attention to his duties. He had even taken care to pack Cal's battered old chain mail and the little wooden practice sword he found amongst Cal's belongings.

Elizebith of Morea was not happy, but she was relieved. Ever since the audience with the king, Cal had seemed like his own, old self again, as though some subtle madness had been lifted from him. He had even tried, in his way, to patch up the rift between them. He had complimented her in the presence of King Alfred and shown her small courtesies she had long since learned not to expect from him. In return, Bith had moderated her attitude toward Cal, trying to rekindle an easier-going friendship. She did not pretend to understand how men could be such fools, particularly about women, but was near to convincing herself that it would be better to accept and live with the fact that they were fools than to try to change them. She harbored grave doubts about the coming battle, and graver doubts still about how her limited skills with magic could contribute to victory. But she would do her best; more than that not even Vili could reasonably ask.

Hathor was happy because Bith seemed happier. He was also pleased with the shining new great axe presented to him by the king, and treated with silver by Endril. It seemed to

Hathor that everything was going much better than it had been, and probably as well as could be expected. He saw no contradiction between his continued belief that Vili was at least interested in their quest and his utter certainty that they were all doomed to die.

Even Endril put on a show of cheerfulness. The elf quipped as of old with Bith and Cal, teased Hathor, and even amused himself by piping a few merry airs. This he did to help all maintain their courage and confidence. In his heart, Endril knew, more than anyone else, the magnitude of the struggle they would soon undertake.

The host slowly wound its way northward along the steep mountain roads, heading toward the great pass. There, the road would descend steeply to the valley at the foot of the Bloody Range. The distance the army had to cover was short in terms of miles, but long in terms of time. A small group of riders could have made the journey in two to three days; it took an army on foot eight to reach the pass high in the windswept mountains. On the evening of that eighth day, while Cal and Bith supped in the king's tent, the knights speculated eagerly on the prospects of battle, and the men of the fyrd fought the chill of the snowy ground with small fires, Endril slipped away alone. His cloak and hood pulled tight to protect himself from the biting, chill winds, the elf ascended to the crest of the pass and looked out into the dusk at the field of battle ahead.

Directly before him the ground dropped steeply, a full three thousand feet to the valley below. That valley marked the northern border of Trondholm. The army, he judged, would take a full day to make its descent. The trail meandered back and forth across the face of the mountain as it wound its way down. Fortunately, the heavy forest here screened the trail from the view of anyone to the north. Unless the enemy used flying creatures to observe from the air, an element of surprise could be acheived.

Next, the elf looked far away to the northwest. There, in the dim twilight, he could see the swirling edge of the Dark Lord's Mistwall where it actually touched the Trondholm border. But the elf's mind was not truly on the Mistwall. His gaze moved from west to east. He saw the Mistwall curled away to the north, bending back behind the massive collection of peaks that reared directly in front of him, four or five miles away across the valley. He let his eyes come to rest on the Bloody Range.

Once again, as happened to him so often of late, the elf's memories merged with his present perceptions. He saw the Bloody Range not as it was, but as it had been, on a harrowing day in the distant past. He heard the screams of enraged, wounded, dying men echoing from those barren, foul colored peaks. In the growing darkness, he could see banners snapping in the cold wind, hear the clash of steel on steel, and notice the twanging sound of a thousand elven bowstrings released at once. He could even smell the spilled warm blood of orcs and men, dwarves and elves, and other creatures so foul his stomach lurched. Before his eyes the battle raged again, continuing on and on, the dead piling so high the living were hard pressed to keep a footing on the gore-soaked slopes. The forces of light and darkness were evenly matched; neither could gain an advantage. Even the bursts of magic that dotted the air were balanced: a hail of fireballs swept from east to west, answered by a trembling of the ground and the collapse of whole slabs of granite behind the mages who launched those orbs of flame.

How long ago had it been? Seven centuries, or eight? It did not matter. On that day long ago Endril had done what had to be done. He had done the one thing that could defeat his own kinsman, Malendor, and the hosts of living dead who fought at Malendor's side. From that day, so many centuries ago, to this, he had paid a price for that deed.

Would he, Endril wondered, have to do it again?

He believed that across the valley, deep beneath the now-still slopes of the Bloody Range, Malendor wondered, too.

As the small army wound its way down the face of the mountain, Cal, Endril, Alfred, and the more pride ridden of the knights made plans for the coming battle. From rocky overlooks they could spy out the plain of the valley below, and Endril, drawing upon memories centuries old, pointed to the mouths of three tiny caverns at the foot of the Bloody Range—places from which the Dark Lord's columns could be expected to emerge. The enemy troops would need a full day to assemble themselves and reorder for the trek across Trondholm's border and up to the pass. At the moment, there was no sign of any activity whatsoever on the forbidding slopes; the forces of Trondholm had arrived before their foes.

"This will be butcher's work," Cal commented as he looked down upon the area indicated by Endril. "We will slaughter them in droves."

"Exactly how?" one of the knights asked gruffly.

"We should deploy in a great semicircle in front of the cavern mouths," Cal said coolly. "We can put masses of archers on the flanks, with their own flanks protected by the rising wall of the Bloody Range itself." Cal stooped down and began drawing a diagram so all could visualize his plan. "Our footmen, armed with sword and spear, deploy in battle line here, directly in front of the cavern mouths, with their flanks resting on the archers. Our knights and mounted retainers we divide into two groups of about one hundred each, held back on each side behind the seam between the footmen and the archers."

"I see your plan," King Alfred interrupted. "As their columns emerge, we allow two to three thousand at a time to march unmolested out of the caverns. They'll still be in march order, not ready to fight. Then, a hail of archery . . ."

"Interrupts the flow of men, shutting off the mouths of the caverns," Cal continued for him. "The men who have already emerged into the valley will be milling about in confusion. Our foot can charge and slaughter them. Then, we slow our archery volleys, and let more of the enemy emerge. At any given time, we control the number of enemy that can actually be used against us."

"Also," Endril added, "our fire at the cavern mouths will help prevent accurate word of what is happening from being passed back along the ranks. It will take time for their commanders to realize their columns are marching into a killing zone."

"Exactly," Cal agreed. "Our mounted troops we hold as a reserve, either to seal any breach they make in our lines, or to pursue."

"I don't relish being a reserve," one of the knights blustered. "The duty of a knight is to fight, not to watch the fyrd slaughter our enemies for us."

"Is it not also the duty of a knight," Alfred said sternly, "to obey his king?"

"But, sire," the knight protested, "the glory of the victory—"

"Will be shared by all the army," the king snapped.

"Do not forget, noble knight," Endril added, "there may well be other foes to face once the sun has set on the day of battle."

"One more thing, though," the king said. "The Dark Lord has spies everywhere. Even the few villages we passed through on our progress here contained members of this cult, the Friends of Eternal Life. Naturally, we have practiced march security and even spread a false tale in the villages as we passed. But what if we have not achieved surprise?"

"Then we will have to fight them in the night," Endril replied. "And they will attack not with men, but with the living dead."

Malendor breathed a mighty curse on all things, living and dead, that defied his will and frustrated his plans. The Dark Lord's main army, scheduled to march through the passageways beneath the Ochre Mountain en route to Trondholm, was two days late. Worse, the king of Trondholm was reported to have led a force of men due north toward the kingdom's border. Their route would place them directly in the path the Dark Lord's human army was to use. It was possible that the Trondholm force had already arrived at the border. If so, Malendor's entire plan would have to be revised, thanks to the incompetence of some moronic army subordinate.

The dark elf fingered the black stone that was his source of power and control over all the undead. As soon as dusk had fallen, he had sent twenty wights, airborne on wyverns, to scout the mountain passes and back trails that could offer an army passage from Trondholm to the Ochre Mountain. Now Malendor closed his eyes, focused his mind, and reached out to the wights one by one. As his power touched each of the creatures, he was able to see through their eyes.

Malendor concentrated deeply. It took a moment for his mind to adjust to the images he received, for the wights saw the world in shades of black, white, and gray only, and always with the colors reversed. Dark objects appeared light, light objects dark. Confusion could result if one was not careful. . . .

There! What was that? Malendor brought all his will to bear on the wight whose eyes he was using. Responding to what it felt as a kind of instinctual urge, the wight guided its wyvern downward. Malendor could feel the undead creature's excitement rise as—there it was! A fire! Then another—then another. There was a host encamped at the foot of Trondholm's mountains, just across the valley. Malendor released his mind from the wight.

"What troubles you, my love?" a voice rasped behind him.

Yvaine glided to stand behind the dark elf. He had not heard her enter, so intense was his concentration. Malendor cursed aloud again. He should have heard her, should have known she was there, should have felt her presence while she was yet hundreds of yards distant. Maintaining control over an entire army of undead creatures, even through the power of the black stone, was taxing his abilities. When added complications arose to demand his attention, small details escaped his notice. This could lead to disaster yet!

"What troubles me is the incompetent stupidity of men!" Malendor shouted. "The Dark Lord's forces have only just arrived here beneath the mountain. They are two days late. King Alfred's force awaits them in the valley beyond. If they march forth tomorrow at first light, as their human commander insists they must, they will be slaughtered piecemeal in an ambush."

"Then send forth your own army, your thousands of undead, now. The humans could not possibly defeat them," Yvaine said. She glanced nervously around Malendor's study, her fangs protruding.

"You have not fed yet tonight, I see," Malendor said with genuine contempt and malice. How disgusting even the vampires were, despite their brilliant minds and great powers. Always they were distracted by the constant hunger for blood.

"No. You have not yet sent me my treat," Yvaine said, evil resentment in her own guttural voice.

"Blood has become scarce these past days, for there have been many to feed. I will tend to your needs shortly."

"After you launch your attack?"

"I would if I could. But I cannot attack yet. The zombies have been given careful instructions—all pertaining to an attack on one specific place. The battlefield is now not there, but at my own front door. It will take at least one full night to drum the new instructions into their dead minds."

Yvaine nodded. She had practiced controlling animated corpses herself. One had to carefully teach them every movement if they were to carry out any role other than staggering forward to attack everything in sight.

"Then what will you do?" she asked. She had little interest in Malendor's military plans, but the sooner he decided on a course of action, the sooner the burning hunger within her could be satisfied.

"I don't know. I keep suffering interruptions," Malendor said with a glance that commanded her to leave.

Yvaine reluctantly moved toward the study door.

"Why not," she said as she left the room, "allow the incompetent humans to march out to defeat tomorrow? Then, in the night, your own forces can attack the Trondholm army in the midst of their victory celebration. You will succeed where the Dark Lord's other servants have failed."

Of course, Malendor realized. *She is correct.* Why had he not thought of this? The strain of maintaining control over thousands of undead was greater than he had remembered. Let the Dark Lord's human army march to its death. Their corpses could swell his own ranks after sunset. Malendor chuckled to himself as he turned his attention to the feeding of his vampiress—and himself.

"Dowse those fires!" Endril whispered hoarsely to the assemblage of fyrd who huddled to warm themselves. "Do you want every fiend from a thousand hells to see where you are?"

Already Endril had heard the flapping of wyvern wings high overhead. The army was probably spotted, its advantage of surprise destroyed. Still, there was every reason to continue to take precautions. Perhaps the message would fail to be relayed by the enemy's lookouts; in war, the unexpected was to be expected. Sometimes, the unexpected could be good as well as bad.

Worried, the elf went to Cal's side and shook the human awake.

"I think they have spotted our force. I heard wyverns overhead."

Cal was instantly awake and alert.

"What would be the first sign of an attack?" he asked in a whisper.

"Men dying silently in their sleep," Endril replied, a dreamy look in his eyes. "The shadows would come first; silent, inky pools of cold blackness flitting with the speed of thought across the ground, draining life from all they touched. I have seen this before."

"What hour is it?" Cal asked.

"Two hours until sunrise."

"Let's rouse the men and move into position now. I doubt that most are sleeping well anyway. The eve of battle is often a sleepless night."

Endril nodded, and within the hour, the men of Trondholm were marching quietly across the valley. By first light, every foot soldier was hidden in the tall summer grass beyond the entrances to the caverns that led into the heart of the Bloody Range. The cavalry stood in ranks in their assigned positions, the only Trondholm forces visible on the field.

"Again, I must urge you to caution," Malendor said to the plate-armored man who sat astride a monstrous warhorse near the mouth of the cavern. Outside that entrance, both could see the open valley stretching for miles ahead. There was nothing in that valley save the tall grass common to the region. Beyond the valley, the mountains of Trondholm reared.

"I have intelligence that the enemy force is very near. You may be marching into danger," Malendor told the human.

The black elf's words were carefully calculated to goad the arrogant man into rashness.

"Do you think we fear danger?" the man barked. "Whatever forces the Trondholmers can raise my heavy cavalry can brush aside."

"At least I could send out some scouts, airborne on my wyverns," Malendor suggested. He knew full well that this particular human detested the flying beasts.

"We've no need of your flying beasts or your undead zombies. We are men, as dedicated to the service of the Dark Lord in our own way as you are in yours. You delay us from our duty."

"Then go forth to victory," Malendor said with a slight bow of his head. He turned himself to a fog before the man's eyes and in an instant was back in his study, relishing the failure the human was about to experience.

"Now, strike, Trondholmers. Strike well and hard—to my greater glory!"

• • •

The rising sun glinted off the great crested helms of the Dark Lord's heavy knights. Their huge black steeds thundered forth in three columns from the cavern mouths in the side of the Bloody Range. The men had been carefully picked for size, strength, and skill at arms. None was less than six feet in height—giants among the normal range of men. Each wore a full suit of black steel armor, carefully fluted and fashioned to deflect both blade and arrow. Each carried a great shield, a heavy lance, and wore a bastard sword at his side. The full helmets of the men were adorned with horsehair crests in brilliant colors: red, gold, blue, silver, and black. Among them rode smaller men, more lightly armored, bearing standards, with drums and trumpets strapped among the gear on their smaller horses.

Cal gazed in admiration as these fighters trotted into the ambush he had prepared.

"It is a shame these men serve the cause of evil. They are mighty warriors," he remarked to Endril and Bith.

"Look there," Bith replied, pointing. "They have spotted our small cavalry forces."

The leaders of the western and eastern columns led their men into a smooth turn toward the nearest of King Alfred's mounted troops, clearly visible at a distance of some one thousand yards across the valley floor. The Trondholm archers and infantry lay still upon the earth, their presence hidden by the high wild grass.

Cal brought his mount up beside that of the king.

"Sire, it is almost time. I count six hundred of them now."

"I wonder how many such cavalry they have," the king said, a trace of anxiety in his voice.

"I doubt much more," Cal said steadily. "Infantry are the mainstay of the Dark Lord's forces. The heavy cavalry are his best troops, and they demand the honor of leading every advance."

"Not unlike the knights of Trondholm," King Alfred responded.

The king raised a great red banner in his right arm, and with a sudden motion, lowered it to the ground.

Two hundred Trondholm troops armed with heavy cross-bows rose as a single man. They stood in three ranks, one group on either side of the enemy cavalry, very near the cavern mouths. Each rank fired a volley a turn. The swift, heavy bolts found many targets. Horses whinnied and reared in sudden pain; several fell crashing to the earth, dead before they hit the ground. Men cried out in pain as well. The deadly hail of bolts, fired with great force at close range, penetrated even the fine, heavy armor of these warriors.

The column leaders reined in their horses, halting for an instant to assess the new situation. As they paused, the two rear ranks of each group of crossbowmen reloaded. The front rank hurled spiked caltrops out to their front, then began to plant sharp-pointed wooden stakes before them and by their flanks.

This manuever was a gamble; Cal had planned it, judging that when the enemy brought out his cavalry, they would be confused for a time by our archers. Still, the bowmen would barely have time to prepare their defenses before the horsemen could form up to charge them. . . .

The enemy commanders proved to be of varying skill. The man leading the westernmost column was swift to respond. He ordered a quick right turn, and his column suddenly became two lines of horsemen facing the nearest archers. The commander closed his beaver, leveled his lance, and with a great cry, charged toward the Trondholm crossbows. His men followed fearlessly.

The bowmen dropped their remaining stakes and quickly re-formed their ranks. By the time they were ready, the horsemen were almost upon them. But then the front line of the charging knights wavered. The horses had reached the caltrops—bundles of huge wooden spikes extending upward from the ground in all directions. Try as they might, the knights could not urge their steeds directly over these barriers. Horses swerved and reared, and the heavily armored men fought to keep their mounts. Lances fell useless on the ground. Moments later, the second rank of charging horsemen plowed into the first. The result was mass confusion.

Even so, many of the knights were able to regain control of their horses, and they plunged forward, armed with sword and mace. Seconds before the first made contact with the first line of bowmen, the three ranks of crossbows fired as one. With shrieks of pain and howls of rage, the attack faltered. A few knights, infuriated, left their mounts to wade into the bowmen on foot, but the nimbler bowmen, unencumbered by armor, turned and ran.

The leader of the eastern column of the Dark Lord's cavalry was confused; his men milled helplessly in the arrow storm that assailed them, awaiting orders. The central column halted in the middle of the field; their leader was uncertain which direction to take. Should he reinforce the charge on the west or go to the aid of his fellows to the east?

From his position on the east flank, with half his own horsemen, King Alfred neatly judged the situation. "Green flag," the king commanded without hesitation. A servant handed the king a great green banner on a tall pole. The king held the banner high, then dropped it to the ground. Across the field, the western block of Trondholm's cavalry reserve launched a savage countercharge.

The Trondholm bowmen on the western flank of the field ran around and behind their own oncoming horses. The Trondholm knights, only one hundred strong, crashed into the milling, confused mass of the Dark Lord's knights. A grand melee ensued.

Meanwhile, from the posts by King Alfred, Cal and Endril carefully watched the cavern mouths. As they had hoped, the heads of columns of infantry had appeared, and these were halted, as their leaders tried to assess the situation.

"Half the spearmen now, I think," Cal said. The elf nodded. King Alfred agreed. The signal was passed, and at the southern end of the field a line of Trondholm swordsmen and spearmen stood up from hiding in the tall grass. Appearing as if from nowhere, they advanced steadily against all three columns of enemy horses.

The melee lasted a full twenty minutes, but the Dark Lord's fine cavalry could not prevail. Taken in three separated sections, harassed by crossbow bolts, charged in front and flank, they were doomed. The men fought with true ferocity and skill, but, unable to form or charge properly, save for the one column, they were more hampered than helped by their heavy equipment. The Trondholm infantry used spears and bills to strike down their foes, and short swords to pierce their heavy armor.

As the Dark Lord's horsemen fell, his infantry finally attempted to advance to their aid.

Once again, the crossbows began shooting. Those on the western flank of the field had regained their original positions, and against more lightly armored infantry their short-range volleys had a devastating effect. More and more of the enemy debauched onto the field, only to be riddled by bolts, lose cohesion, and disintegrate into a mass of wildly fleeing men.

"I believe it is time to add to their panic and confusion," Bith suggested as the battle raged on, and more and more of the enemy milled about aimlessly in the great killing zone. The enchantress waved her arms and recited an incantation. A tiny spark of flame leaped from her fingertip, speeding into the midst of the confused mass of enemy troops, its diameter increasing dramatically as it moved. In the center of the field it formed a huge ball of flame fully six feet across, and then exploded with violent force, hurling men into the air and bathing them in sticky flames.

In ninety minutes, the victory of Trondholm was complete. Cal and Endril judged that fully five thousand enemy had marched onto the grassy field. Now, no more troops appeared at the mouths of the caverns, and as the men of Trondholm grew weary from the constant exertion of mortal combat, more and more of the enemy were working through the Trondholm ranks, fleeing in panic toward the shelter of the Mistwall some miles away to the northwest.

"We are winning," Hathor said simply to Cal.

"Yes, and it is time to make the victory complete," Cal replied. A steely look of murderous intent suddenly blazed from Cal's eyes. "Olaf," he called, "bring me the sword!"

His lackey instantly appeared. In one hand he carried the runesword; in the other, he held the little wooden practice sword.

Cal laughed as he saw the wooden weapon. He handed Olaf the long sword presented him by the king, and raised the great runesword high in the air. Olaf, uncertain what to do, as his lord suddenly seemed to be overcome by strange emotions, tucked the wooden sword into the empty scabbard at Cal's side.

With a sudden scream, Cal charged into the fray, his great weapon rising and falling and rising and falling again as he hacked his way through the mass of terrified men, heading toward his own western lines.

"Cal! No!," Endril shouted, suddenly aware of what Cal was doing.

"What is it, Endril?" Bith asked.

"The fool! His blood lust is up. He'll pursue them, and we'll miss our opportunity to get inside those caverns!"

"Then after him!" Hathor roared, and off charged the great troll.

Bith and Endril looked helplessly at one another.

"After you, my lady," Endril quipped.

"We shall return, my lord king, after your victory is sealed," Bith called to Alfred as she, in turn, galloped into the battle with Endril close behind her.

CHAPTER
17

Into the Mistwall

Cal galloped forward, slaying anything that moved within the reach of his sword. The enchanted blade seemed to sing a high-pitched song of slaughter as it cleaved the air and sliced effortlessly through leather, metal, skin, bone, and sinew.

Cal shouted again, this time with pure glee. He had experienced battle frenzy before, but never like this. Never before had he taken such a pure joy in dealing death to his foes. And never before had he laughed to see heads fly through the air, or hapless men trying helplessly to stuff their own intestines back inside themselves.

On he pressed in frenzied ecstasy, until he had fought his way completely through to his own lines on the western flank, and then found himself pursuing the fleeing enemy beyond.

Ahead, near the false horizon formed by the Mistwall itself, Cal saw one of the surviving knights of the Dark Lord riding for his life toward that swirling wall of fog.

"He's mine!" Cal cried, his blood rising yet again. He dug his spurs into the flanks of his tiring mount, and again the great warhorse stretched to a full gallop.

The runesword streamed blood and gore as horse and rider tore across the plain of the valley. Far behind Cal, vain voices called his name, urging him to return. But Cal, intent upon the death of his newfound prey, never heard them.

The fleeing knight reined to a stop and turned to survey the scene behind him. He saw his pursuer in gleaming armor, the royal standard of Trondholm on the great shield. The black rider turned his mount again toward the wall of mist ahead and rode hard. His horse was tiring, but he just might make the safety of the Mistwall before his pursuer closed.

Cal was not thirty yards behind when horse and rider were suddenly swallowed by the barrier that divided the normal earth from the domain where the Dark Lord's rule was absolute.

Cal did not hesitate for an instant. His mount never slowed for a single step. Forward they plunged together into the unknown.

And suddenly, Cal was all but blinded. He could see nothing in the dense mist, nothing but swirling, mottled colors. His sense of direction vanished as quickly as his vision. On he rode, but whether or not he still pursued his foe he did not know. Finally, his horse slowed of its own accord, and then stopped, its great flanks heaving as it gulped the strange air.

Cal's blood lust was strong. Not even the strange, almost nauseating swirl of nothingness all around him quelled his desire to kill. He struggled to see something, anything, in the infuriating fog. At length, he thought he spied a dark, shadowy, armored form standing some distance from himself.

"Caltus Talienson," called a deep, low voice, not unlike the voice of the god Vili himself.

"I am Caltus Talienson. If you are of the Dark Lord's horde, stand and fight," Cal shouted back.

The figure seemed more clear to Cal's vision now. It stood its ground and drew a great blade, black as pitch, as black as the armor it wore, as black as the horsehair crest atop its great beavered helm.

"Come for me," the voice boomed. "I am what you seek."

Without a further word Cal dismounted, raised his sword, and charged.

Steel rang on steel as Cal's blade crashed against the black blade of his enemy. Pain shot up Cal's right arm from the shock of the impact. The man was incredibly strong, and his swing knocked Cal's blade aside.

Cal stepped back, parrying a quick thrust that followed the initial contact with lightning speed. Five times more in less than three seconds the great blades rang as they crashed together, neither man able to find an opening or land a blow. As if by mutual consent, each paused, studying the other.

"You fight well," the black knight's voice boomed around Cal.

"As do you," Cal acknowledged. "But you fight for evil, and death must be your lot!"

Even as he spoke, Cal renewed his attack, slashing, thrusting, striking up and down and side to side with dizzying speed. Yet still his enemy parried every strike, and struck back again. Cal's runesword blocked the series of blows rained upon him by the man in black.

The knight backed off three paces and lowered his blade, leaning upon the hilt. Cal welcomed the respite. His breath came now in great gasps. Stinging sweat streamed into his eyes. His hands were numb from the constant stinging of blow after blow against his foe's black sword. His arms ached from exertion.

Cal decided to try a different tactic.

With a sudden cry he lunged forward, swinging the runesword as if for a normal blow. His foe, as he expected, raised his own blade to parry. Cal swung around full circle, and as he came around again, raised his left arm so that it crashed full force into his opponent's chest.

"Unnhh!" the black knight grunted, toppling over backward. Cal steadied himself on his own feet, and the runesword sliced upward through the fog, poised to plunge down into the fallen enemy's breast. But it was not to be.

The black knight's legs kicked upward, wrapping around Cal's behind the knees, pulling the youth down.

The two rolled over and over, fists beating with frustration against each other's armor. At length Cal, on his back, summoned all his strength and literally tossed the black knight's body up and off of him. Both men regained their footing at the same time.

"Why fight me, Caltus Talienson?" the knight queried as again both men paused, breathing heavily. "You do not want to slay me."

"Indeed, that is clearly my intention," Cal replied.

"But you do not know me."

"You fight for the Dark Lord. That is all I need know."

"You cannot slay me, ever," the black knight said, his voice low but strangely soft.

"Bold words," Cal panted. "What basis have you for that claim?"

"Your love," the knight replied, suddenly reaching up, raising his beaver, then tossing his great helmet aside.

Cal gasped. It was Yvaine. She smiled at him her most winning smile, the smile he remembered so well from that day long ago in the courtyard garden, the smile of a goddess in love. Then she lunged toward him.

More from instinct than intent, Cal raised his sword in a purely defensive move, and the onrushing figure impaled itself on the magic blade.

A horrid gurgling sound emerged from Yvaine's mouth. Her blue eyes shot wide open with shock. Blood mixed with spittle bubbled from her mouth.

"Caltus, my love," she said plaintively, falling dead upon his sword.

Cal screamed in pure horror.

Hastily, Elizabeth traced a circle in the ground she felt beneath her feet. Once again she repeated the words the god had taught her in the night, and once again she felt the power of pure goodness surround her.

Hathor and Endril saw a flash of light, and their vision cleared. They stood very close to Bith, well within the circle she had traced. Within its diameter, the mist was gone, and all could be clearly seen.

The three had pursued Cal into the Mistwall, fearful for his life and certain they would need his prowess for the greater battle yet to be fought. For, as Endril had explained hastily to the other two, the leader of the Friends of Eternal Life had his stronghold beneath the Bloody Range. If they were to find Yvaine, that stronghold must be penetrated.

"Cal," Bith called. Endril and Hathor called in turn. For a moment they heard nothing in response. Then, from somewhere, they heard a human scream of such pure horror and distress that even Hathor's hair prickled up on his great arms.

"That's Cal," Bith said. Without hesitation the enchantress walked out of the safety of the magic circle, seeking her warrior companion in the depths of the mist.

They found Cal standing frozen like a statue, his sword in his hands, and a dead knight impaled upon its blade. Cal stood screaming over and over again, as if under some hideous magical spell that forbade him any other action.

Wordlessly, Bith and Endril took Cal by his arms. Hathor removed the runesword from Cal's grasp, then picked up the dead knight and tossed the body over his shoulder. Together, the three guided the still-screaming Cal first to the shelter of the magic circle, and then out of the Mistwall, back to the plain of the valley.

CHAPTER
18

Heart Ruined

Cal collapsed in the grass. His three companions gathered around him, uncertain how to proceed.

"Vili said the girl was at the Bloody Range," Bith said. "We'll never have a better opportunity to enter those caverns than right now, while the enemy is in disarray."

Beyond them, the army of Trondholm celebrated its victory. Here and there across the plain, soldiers were still rounding a few of the remnants of the Dark Lord's forces. Prisoners were being taken; most of the men of Trondholm had had enough of slaughter for one day.

"And we must move quickly," Endril urged. "Already the sun is well advanced in the sky. If we do not defeat . . . the leader of the cult before nightfall, his undead minions can still be unleashed."

"But we fought undead in daylight before," Hathor commented.

"Yes. But their leader is a cunning sort who always plans every detail. He will not move until all his forces can employ their full powers."

Hathor and Bith both stared hard at Endril. He read the question in their eyes.

"I knew him once. Long ago," the elf said.

"Then we must go now. What can we do with Cal?" Hathor asked.

"We need him badly. He is not wounded," Endril observed.

"He still has his sickness," Hathor said.

A long, moaning sob emerged from Cal as he lay in the grass. His startled friends could see the violent shaking of his body, despite the solid plate armor he still wore.

Bith stooped down beside Cal and slipped his helmet from his head. Then she sat, cradling his head in her lap. For several minutes Cal sobbed violently while Bith soothed his cheeks with her hands and wiped his tears on her cloak. As his choking sobs began to subside, Bith spoke.

"Cal," she said softly, "you must tell us what happened."

"Yvaine . . . dead . . . Killed her myself . . ." Cal could only mutter phrases between a combination of renewed sobs and great gasps for air.

"An illusion," Endril said with sudden certainty. "The Mistwall is well known for producing illusions among those who dare to enter it."

"Cal," Bith said, "Yvaine was not in the Mistwall. It was an illusion only, caused by some evil spell, perhaps. See, here is the body of the man you killed."

Cal raised his swollen, red eyes and stared blankly at the corpse of a large knight in black armor.

"Illusion?" he queried. "Only, only an illusion?"

"Come, Cal," Hathor said cheerily. "Your lady is still in the caverns beneath the Bloody Range. Let's go get her."

Hathor's matter-of-fact cheerfulness struck Cal like a tonic. He staggered to his feet.

"Yes, yes, Hathor," he said, a note of hysteria still in his shaking voice. "Let's go get her!"

Seated in his study, Malendor opened his eyes. The time of his revenge was at hand.

The dark elf left his study room, passed through the great cavern room, and turned down one of the endless tunnels that ran beneath the mountain. He strode into a small stone chamber that contained a single coffin, and flipped up the lid.

Touching the black stone at his breast, he uttered a single word.

"Arise," he said.

Yvaine's eyes opened instantly.

"I have not rested the usual time," she complained.

"No matter. All is darkness here; no sunlight will enter to harm you. It is time for you to fulfill your destiny and play your role in my revenge."

"Then the elf comes?"

"Endril comes," Malendor said, nodding and smiling.

"You promised me two things," Yvaine said. A hiss crept into her voice as she spoke; already the hunger was rising within her.

"First, that I would explain to you my plan," Malendor said. "Come to my study, and I will fulfill that promise."

"And the second?"

"Have no fear. Caltus Talienson comes with the elf." *You will have your breakfast, my pet,* he thought, but did not say this.

Outside, the sun reddened as it began its daily descent toward the western horizon. The four companions stood near the entrance to a cave that stretched as far as they could see into the heart of the huge Bloody Range.

"We must find and defeat the leader of the cult before sunset," Endril said quietly.

"And we must find Yvaine. Surely she is here, a prisoner of the source of this evil," Cal stated. He was not yet fully in his right mind, but the instincts of duty and combat drew him on, as did some deeper compulsion he could not identify.

"There could be many tunnels beneath so large a range of peaks," Hathor said. "We could search for days."

"I know the way," Endril said. "I have been here before."

Bith raised an eyebrow but said nothing.

"Then let's go," Cal said, plunging forward into the darkness.

Endril and Hathor both shot out arms to restrain the youth.

"First, Cal, we must prepare," Hathor cautioned.

Endril quickly ran down their list of weapons, all treated with silver, save for the runesword, which could harm anything by virtue of its powerful magic. All four carried oil, matches, and rope as well. To each Endril handed a flask containing a clear liquid.

"Holy water, blessed by the holy ones of Odin in Trondholm," Endril explained. "A gift to us from King Alfred."

"Better he should give us troops," Hathor said.

"No, friend. What we must do is best done by us alone. Common humans would stand little chance in these tunnels."

As do we, Hathor thought.

"I have already prepared myself to see the aura of any magical traps," Bith said. "I will stop us if I see such dangers."

Bith began to chant. In her hands she held tiny bits of dried herbs and mixtures of strange powders. Around her waist she had tied a rope. As she continued her incantation, Endril tied it in turn around Hathor, then Cal, then himself.

"This will keep us together," he whispered.

Bith ended her enchantment, and suddenly the four companions vanished from sight.

"And now for silence," Bith's voice said. She recited a second spell, and from that moment the only contact between the four was the pressure on the invisible rope that linked them.

After a moment, a gentle tug indicated to Cal, Hathor, and Bith that Endril was moving forward. Together, the four entered the darkness of the tunnels.

• • •

"You were the key," Malendor said to Yvaine as he settled back in his favorite chair in his secret study room. "You, and the sword young Talienson carries. I knew Endril would never come here willingly. He knows the danger is too great and perhaps fears what he might be tempted to do to avert that danger."

"And that is what?" Yvaine asked, eagerly.

"That is unimportant. What matters is that your love for Caltus, and his for you, enabled me to change the enchantment on that magic blade of his. From the time he received it back, I have controlled almost every move he's made. So long as it is in his hands, I can read his thoughts and influence his decisions.

"It was not difficult, of course, to encourage his natural desire to find you. And I knew that where he came, the others would follow. Impersonating their pathetic god added an aesthetic touch to the scheme.

"And even now, I can see through Talienson's eyes. They have entered the first corridor. They come invisibly, silently. They fear the mob of troops they know must still be within these tunnels, and Endril fears creatures such as yourself, whom he knows I can control."

"If they are here, what is my part to play?" Yvaine asked. "Remember, you promised me Talienson forever."

"Yes, yes. Do your part and you shall have him."

"What is my part?"

"Simply this. Convince Caltus Talienson to slay Endril for me. I want Endril to know that he has placed his friends under my power, and to know the pain of betrayal by them as he dies."

"Will you keep him, then, as an undead?"

"No," Malendor said curtly. He did not add that to attempt to do so would be, perhaps, too dangerous. . . .

"Cal will do as I command him. He truly loves me, you know." The vampiress enjoyed the thought that the human's love might make Malendor feel jealousy.

"I think he will. He had an experience earlier today, arranged by me, that will make him more, let us say, pliable in your hands."

"What of the other two?"

"They are unimportant, so long as Endril sees them die. Perhaps I'll have their corpses dance a jig for him before Talienson slits his throat."

Malendor sat back, relaxed, confident, and expectant. He slipped two rings on his long fingers and waited, watching the door.

Endril proceeded cautiously but swiftly, his memory not failing him. Well did he know the way to the great throne room, where once his kinsman, Malendor, had sat in glory.

The tunnels were thronged with men and beasts. Confusion reigned, as the Dark Lord's remaining forces attempted to reorganize in an environment that was strange and unnatural to men.

Endril quickly realized that the undead creatures under Malendor's control would have to be kept in a different area. Even with Malendor's power, the creatures would be impossible to hold in check in the presence of hundreds of living men. With luck, Endril could lead his companions straight to the great throne room without encountering any of the living dead.

Cal's excitement grew as they plunged deeper and deeper into the tunnel complex. Soon, very soon, he sensed, he would see Yvaine. Then he would hold her in his arms and never let her go. As for her abductor . . .

Bith was extremely worried. The spell she had cast before entering these tunnels should have enabled her to see the aura of any magic whatsoever. Yet there was nothing to be seen. What kind of powerful high priest would not have magical traps and guards along the approach to his stronghold?

Hathor merely hoped that none of the many men in the tunnels, some of whom he could reach out and touch as he walked past, would smell him and raise an alarm. Humans were so touchy about troll odors. . . .

Endril stopped. Directly ahead, the great throne room was empty. The elf bravely suppressed a flood of memories as he scanned the far reaches of the room for any sign of a creature, living or dead. There was nothing.

Boldly, Endril crossed the floor and started to climb the long stone staircase toward the throne. His three companions followed. Cal's excitement was near the boiling point; he could feel the battle frenzy rising within him.

At the top of the stairs at last, Endril paused again. His human companions would need a moment to rest after the climb. And they were very near their goal.

Cal, forging ahead, his mind almost blank as the urge to combat grew overpowering, bumped into Endril from behind.

With such an unceremonious beginning, I again confront my kinsman, Endril thought. The elf led the way behind the throne. He carefully ran his hand along stone wall, feeling for a certain place. . . .

There.

Endril took a deep breath and touched the slight depression in the stone surface three times. Silently, a portion of the wall opened inward, and Endril looked into the eyes of Malendor.

"Welcome, Endril. I have awaited our reunion with some . . . anticipation," Malendor said dryly as the door slid open. In his mind, the dark elf could see himself through Cal's eyes. He could feel the terrific hatred of the youth. Perfect, he thought. Perfect.

"I have arranged a little surprise for you, Endril. What more perfect gift for an elf than a vampiric orc?"

Malendor touched the black stone at his breast, and from within a standing coffin in a back corner of his study, Gobslobble, the hapless orc, burst forth.

"Attack," Malendor commanded. "They are invisible, but they are there."

"I smell their blood," Gobslobble roared.

The transformed orc charged forward, hideous fangs protruding from beneath his hoggish snout. Endril dodged to one side; the thing charged straight through the door and into Cal, who, despite all his desperate longing for battle, was caught unawares by this latest horror. The youth tumbled to the floor. Hathor let out a roar that could not be heard, and raised his huge axe. His tremendous blow drove the blade with faultless skill edge first toward the back of Gobslobble's neck. To Hathor's surprise, the blade was turned by the orc's hide, and Hathor suddenly became visible.

Within two more seconds Gobslobble was truly dead. Cal's enchanted sword severed his head from his neck, even as Endril jammed the wooden shaft of an arrow into the orc's breast and Bith dashed holy water on the obscene creature's body. Now all four were visible, and the magical silence was broken as well.

"Now it is your turn," Cal called to Malendor, "for you, I perceive, are the source of all the evil that has befallen . . ."

Cal stopped in midsentence as Yvaine stepped into view.

She was alive! And never had she appeared more beautiful. Her hair glowed in the sputtering torchlight. Her soft skin invited his caress, and love shone from her blue eyes.

"Cal," she said, her voice as sweet as elven song, "at last you've come for me."

"Yvaine!" Cal rushed to her side, unopposed by Malendor, who remained seated, seemingly unconcerned.

"Ah, Endril, what a touching reunion. Don't you agree?" the black elf taunted.

Bith stared at the woman who had won Cal's heart. What she saw she did not let register on her face. She began to whisper the words of a simple spell.

Cal swept Yvaine into his arms, enfolding her gently, as though she were a fragile, glass butterfly that could break at the slightest touch.

"Yvaine, how I have sought you! Are you well? Have you been harmed?"

"No, Cal, I am not harmed," she replied, still holding his eyes with her own. "I am well, and I can be yours forever if you but will it."

"I will it," Cal said with certainty.

Yvaine pressed her cheek against Cal's neck and whispered in his ear.

Cal turned his head quickly to look at Endril, hatred flashing in his eyes. His hand raised his sword.

At that instant, Bith finished muttering her enchantment.

Before Cal could strike, from the corner of his eye he saw Yvaine suddenly transformed. He looked again into her eyes and saw death. Her golden hair was dry and stringy. Her once-blue eyes were sunk into her too-pale face, which was contorted with a hellish, gleeful anticipation. Two hideous fangs protruded over her lower lip.

"Kill the elf, and we will be lovers, immortal, together forever. You said you willed it," her voice rasped.

Malendor suddenly stood, rage crossing his own face. While he was watching the revenge play he had so carefully staged, the little human witch had cast one spell and undone all his work! For he instantly recognized that Bith's spell was one that canceled other magic. The illusion of beauty with which he had enhanced Yvaine was gone. But worse, the sword Cal wore had lost the special enchantment Malendor had placed upon it. The Dark Elf's hold over the youth's mind was gone. All his stored magic items, as well, would be worthless, including the rings on his fingers. Only the incredible power of the spell upon his black amulet stone had prevented it, too, from being canceled.

Tears formed in Cal's eyes. His left hand dropped to his sword scabbard. He looked again at Endril, who was staring fearlessly into the eyes of Malendor.

"Kill Endril?" he said, muttering to himself. "Kill Endril?" He looked again into the eyes of the vampiress. His entire body began to shudder.

Cal's left hand closed around the hilt of the little wooden practice sword, placed there earlier by the confused Olaf. Cal's eyes were steady on Yvaine's as he slowly drew the wooden sword.

"Yes, Yvaine," Cal whispered. His eyes closed tightly. Tears began to stream freely down his cheeks. "Yes, I do love you."

Cal brought the point of the wooden sword to rest softly at a point on Yvaine's body just beneath her rib cage.

"And because I love you, I will kill for you," he whispered in her ear. At the same instant, he plunged the wooden sword through her gown, into her flesh. With a violent shove, he drove the blade upward behind her ribs, piercing her heart.

Yvaine screamed. Her scream was the high-pitched, horrifying wail of a staked vampire.

Cal screamed as well. His was the scream of one whose whole reason for being has perished before his eyes.

"You are beaten, Malendor," Endril said softly. "Return beyond the Mistwall, and live."

But Malendor was already chanting a spell, his ability to concentrate on his magic disturbed but not destroyed by his rage.

The words were familiar to Endril.

"Bith, Hathor, out of sight!" Endril shouted.

The troll and the sorceress both ducked back out of sight behind the doorway.

"Die!" screamed Malendor, his incantation finished.

The cold of death ran over and through Endril's body, and for a moment he stood frozen, as though slain on the spot.

Malendor stepped forward, his black eyes wide, waiting for Endril's body to topple. For the spell he had cast was the spell of death itself. It could be resisted only by incredibly powerful beings, or those aided by a god. For a full thirty seconds the Black Elf stared into his kinsman's eyes, awaiting the moment of death.

Bith and Hathor peeked around the corner of the doorframe, their breath held tight as they, too, waited for Endril's death. Bith knew as well as Malendor that the powerful death spell was all but irresistible.

Then Endril spoke, his voice a hoarse, croaking whisper.

"Your spell has failed, Malendor. Go, or you will die."

Malendor howled and hurled himself at Endril in a great leap. In midair his elven form changed to that of a great gray howling wolf. As he fell upon Endril, the powerful jaws snapped tight around the elf's neck.

Hathor moved at once. He ran into the room, smashing table and chairs as his axe hummed through the air. The troll raised the great weapon again and let it fall square upon the canine's back—only to once again see his blow glance aside harmlessly. Undaunted, the red-haired creature hurled himself on the wolf's back, his great arms locking around its belly. With all his might, Hathor pulled on the wolf, at the same time rolling onto his own back.

The wolf's jaws lost their grip on Endril's neck. The creature snarled and frothed at the mouth as it tumbled over in Hathor's arms. Hathor slid his arms upward, toward the beast's neck, and squeezed. . . .

Nothing.

Where once the snarling wolf had been there was nothing but a fine mist that was already taking elven form again.

"Cal!" Bith shouted at the top of her lungs. All this time, Cal had stood, trembling and sobbing, as the blood of Yvaine poured from her body over his hand and arm. His eyes had never left hers.

"Cal!" Bith shouted again. "Use the runesword!"

Malendor materialized fully again, standing directly behind Hathor. With one great sweep of his arm, he knocked the mighty troll backward against the stone wall of the now-demolished room. Hathor thudded against the wall, then crashed to the floor amid the clatter of broken shelves and vials.

Cal turned his head slowly away from Yvaine's dead face. He saw Endril lying in a pool of blood on the littered floor. He saw Hathor trying to stagger to his feet, blood seeping from his sides, where his impact with the wall had broken even the troll's tough hide.

"I will have my revenge!" Malendor hissed. "Talienson! Face me, or be forever called a coward!"

"No, Cal," Bith called. "Don't look in his eyes! Use the runesword!"

Cal let go the dead body of Yvaine. He roared a mighty roar, raised high the runesword, and, staring Malendor straight in the eyes, started to charge across the room.

"Halt, mortal!" Malendor's voice of command boomed. "Slay the elf!"

Cal never paused for an instant. He charged straight ahead two more steps, raised the sword, and with a mighty slash sliced the blade straight through Malendor's body, from head to torso. The blade passed through the Dark Elf and clanged against the stone floor.

For an instant, the Dark Elf and the youthful warrior stared at one another, both in deep shock. Cal could not believe that the powerful runesword had passed harmlessly through his foe's body, leaving not a single scratch. Malendor could not believe that the youth's hatred was so great that even his own powerful, magical gaze could no longer control the youth's mind.

Cal recovered from his shock first. Again he raised the sword and swung, this time a horizontal blow. The blade passed through Malendor's neck, harmlessly.

By now, Hathor had finally staggered to his feet. The troll saw the second sword blow fail to even budge Malendor. He saw the black amulet the creature wore fall to the ground, the gold chain that held it sliced neatly in two by the runesword. He saw Malendor's nervous glance down toward the amulet . . .

And dived.

The troll's hairy hand clasped around the amulet an instant before Malendor's.

"Bith!" Hathor called.

Malendor's iron grip closed on Hathor's arm, and a numbing cold began to spread through the troll's body. His last conscious act in the battle was to summon all his strength and fling the amulet toward the doorway, where Bith stood, helplessly watching her companions being bested.

Bith caught the amulet and ran.

Malendor released his grip on Hathor and lunged for the doorway to pursue her.

"Witch! Touching that will be your death," he shouted, totally beside himself with rage and frustration.

But even while Hathor was still in the Dark Elf's life-draining grasp, Cal was reacting. As Hathor pitched the amulet to Bith, Cal grabbed and unstopped his vial of holy water. Now, he lunged toward Malendor, and as the Dark Elf reached the door, splattered blessed fluid square in the face of the Lord on Earth of the Undead.

Malendor stopped in his tracks and raised his hands involuntarily to his face. Between the Dark Elf's finger, Cal could see the flesh literally begin to boil.

A short distance down the corridor outside the study, Bith stopped. Panting, she studied the amulet. The jet black stone gleamed and glowed with a seeming life of its own. Whatever it was, it was magical, Bith decided, and from Malendor's reaction to her taking it, it must be a source of his power. Immediately, she began an incantation.

"For this, you die," Malendor shrieked at Cal. Just as he had grasped Hathor, the Black Elf grabbed Cal. At the creature's touch, life began to drain from Cal's body. Cold and numbness seeped through his body. The shrieking Black Elf's foul breath was hot in Cal's face; the black eyes, full of hatred, burned into Cal's. The youth's vision began to swim, to dim. . . .

Bith finished her incantation and the living light in the black stone vanished.

Malendor suddenly released Cal, who fell to the floor, his armor clanking on the stone floor.

"No. No! Not back in my body . . . ," Malendor was saying.

Cal, still conscious but unable to think, knew only one thing. This was battle. The foe was before him. He saw

Malendor stumble backward to rest against the wall, a look of surprise and horror on his face. There was his target.

Cal's cold, numb arms raised the runesword yet again. He staggered forward, lurching, almost falling as he whipped the blade through the air.

Malendor's severed head plunked onto the floor at Cal's feet.

Cal grabbed the head by its long black hair and banged it, again and again, against the hard floor.

Bith peered into the room cautiously. She saw the horribly wounded Endril drag his bleeding body over to the unconscious Cal. She saw the elf unwrap Cal's fingers from Malendor's hair. She saw him lift the crushed head, brains leaking down its side, and gently close the cold, dead black eyes.

"Wherever you are, kinsman, know this," the elf whispered. "It was not by my hand. Not by my hand."

CHAPTER
19

Aftermath

Endril piped a mournful tune to himself as he sat in the great brass bed in his quarters at the royal residence in Trondholm. He, Bith, Cal, and Hathor were more than welcome guests there. In fact, they were treated almost as equals of King Alfred himself. Special quarters had been prepared to the tastes of each. Above Endril's head, and around his large, soft bed, potted green plants of all descriptions drank in the sunlight that streamed through the great windows. Some were hung from the broad overhead beams; others were placed among the ornate tables, cabinets, and chairs of finest hardwood that furnished his room.

Endril's sad tune was interrupted by a knock at the door. The hinges creaked as the door opened slightly and Bith peeped in.

"Well, Endril, I see your tune is still mournful," Bith said. "Come, we were victorious. Let us enjoy some cheer from that."

Victorious they had been, and Bith had played a key role in that victory. It was Endril who later explained to her that the black amulet was not only the source of Malendor's power over the undead, but the repository of the Black Elf's own life force. Bith's spell, directed solely at the amulet, had dispelled its enchantment. Malendor's life force had fled to the Black Elf's body, which, without the magical power of the amulet, was simply a normal elven body. Cal's battle lust had done the rest.

With the amulet destroyed, all the undead Malendor had summoned into being were destroyed at once. And with Malendor truly dead, the Friends of Eternal Life gradually disbanded. King Alfred had hastened the demise of the cult by rounding up a few of its more important leaders throughout Trondholm and having them publicly executed for treason.

The four companions had been given heroes' welcomes at the royal residence, and had been there for several weeks, while Cal, Endril, and Hathor recuperated from their wounds.

"You may well be cheerful in victory," Endril replied to Bith. "I do not begrudge you that. But Malendor is forever gone. Certainly he was evil, and his final death was just. But he was my kinsman, and more. I had hoped to avoid this outcome."

"So you knew all along about Malendor and his cult and the power that he had. . . ."

"Yes, Bith. Although I did not know the full nature of his plan. I certainly did not suspect, at least initially, that he had desecrated the runesword and was using it to influence Cal, and us."

"Cal's heart does not heal," Bith said sadly. "He cannot forgive himself for Yvaine's death. With her gone, he feels there is no purpose left in his life."

"I will speak with him," Endril promised. "When my own mourning is over."

"Thank you," Bith said.

"We should thank you," Endril said. "It was your spell that sealed the victory. How did you come to be so well prepared?"

"I have little offensive magic, as you know. I decided it would be best to be well prepared to make the magic of others go away. And as I cast that last spell, I felt something else—some power, or presence, that aided me. . . ."

Endril nodded sagely.

"How are your wounds healing, Cal?" Endril asked. True to his word, he had come to see Cal in his quarters. There, heavy curtains covered the windows, keeping out the light of the sun. Cal slumped in his bed, staring vacantly at the high ceiling.

"Well enough."

"Bith says you are deeply troubled. Sorrow shared is often sorrow eased," Endril said, inviting Cal's confidence.

"Guilt is an enemy I do not know how to fight."

"Guilt?"

"I destroyed something, someone, who was . . . beautiful and wonderful. I destroyed the person I loved the most."

"Malendor destroyed her," Endril said gently, sitting on the edge of Cal's bed. "Not you."

"It was because of my folly that I met her in the first place. If she had not been associated with me, she would never have been touched by Malendor."

"That is true."

Endril's response took Cal by surprise. He had expected some sympathetic statement, not agreement.

"So, I am guilty of her death."

"You are guilty of folly. Malendor is guilty of her death. Stop trying to be a god, responsible for everything."

"A god? What good are the gods? What good has Vili done us? What good have all the gods done for the world?"

"Perhaps some," Endril said, smiling. The elf knew full well that it was not his own power that had resisted Malendor's death spell. Nor was Bith a strong enough mage to have dispelled Malendor's amulet. "We are still alive."

"Perhaps none," Cal rejoined. "Even the runesword is gone. Bith said that it was nowhere to be found when the struggle with Malendor was ended."

"Perhaps the question of the worth of the gods, and the worth of life, depends upon how you choose to see things."

"What do you mean?" Cal asked.

"When you shared a brief time of love with Yvaine, was not the world a wonderful place? Did you not find joy and wonder in everything you saw?"

"Yes."

"And now that she is gone, do you not find only sorrow and bitterness?"

"Yes."

"Surely the world has not changed so much, despite the great events of these months. How you have chosen to see the world has changed," Endril explained. "Besides, how can you hope to understand good and evil and the gods when you cannot yet understand yourself?"

Cal would ponder long on Endril's words.

Hathor, too, pondered as he pounded out bread dough in the bakeries attached to King Alfred's kitchens. The problem that occupied the troll's mind had him truly and deeply perplexed.

King Alfred had been very generous to Bith, Cal, Endril, and himself. For the first time, they had a real reward for their efforts, and genuine wealth at their disposal. Not only had the king given them the use of his residence for as long as they needed, he had actually given them a small chest full of gold coins, gemstones, and jewelry. By Hathor's reckoning, the total value was well over twenty thousand gold coins. And it was this that troubled Hathor deeply.

What on earth, Hathor wondered, would they do with it?